Love or Obsession
A Woman's Touch

A Fiction Novel
By
Brooklyn Phoenix

Love or Obsession:
A Woman's Touch

TM.

Copy written © 2008 BY. Billie Green
Publisher: Alter Ego Publishing
ISBN 978-161658567-9
Edited by Essence Clark
Cover by AC Designs Andrew R. Clifton &
Billie Green

Dedicated to my Grandmother "Auntie Jean" Words cannot express how much you mean to me. You taught me that I could do anything that I put my mind to, and to strive for nothing but the best.

My world will never be the same with out you.

I only hope that I can be nearly as brave and strong as you .

Until we meet again..........

Me

Introduction

*H*ere I am standing in the middle of my kitchen. The moving trucks are outside, the kids are staying with my mother, and I'm surveying the apartment to make sure nothing gets left behind. See this exact moment has been in the works for about a year.

I signed the final paperwork for my new house in Garden City, Long Island. It has always been my dream house: five bedrooms, a pool, two fireplaces, two-car garage, and a wrap-around porch. I imagined myself sipping lemonade while swinging on my porch. This is the home that encouraged me to spend all those years in medical school and all those long nights in the Emergency Room; the home that I always dreamed of for my children and myself. Notice I said children and myself, no significant other that leads me to my story.

Physically I am quite desirable. I'm about 5 feet 9 inches, light skin, slim build, the stereotypical light-skin female. To describe myself any other way, I would say I'm loving, intelligent, sexy, a hard worker, you name it. So why can't I be happy in the love and relationship department? We don't know. I say we, meaning my best friend and myself. By the way I am Anaiyah Williams.

My best friend since kindergarten is Dahlia Richardson, and she's my ride or die chic, my ace in the hole. Hell, anyone from Brooklyn will know exactly what I mean. She's been there since the sun rose, and we have vowed to be there for each other until the sunsets. Not to mention all the free advice I get since she is a psychologist (laughing my ass off)... But she will be the first to tell you, that I need to write a book and here we go.

SIGH..

Chapter 1

Now, I'm moving into this house with so many unanswered questions and undecided issues. See, my problem is I fell in love with a WOMAN. Yes I said a woman... Now how did this happen? Well, I know HOW it happened, but WHY it happened I have no clue. As I told you I have children, three to be exact, so that tells you that I've been with men. Oh yeah, I've been in love with men, long relationships with men and even lived with them. The catch is I also have a child with the woman I fell in love with. Confused yet? Now would I say I'm gay? No, but by the end we will all figure it out.

See why Dahlia loves to talk to me? My experiences are not remotely close to anything that she has read about in a textbook. She's always said that I am way more interesting. All throughout her psychology courses, she compared me to each case. I was her guinea pig. She would always interview me, as if she didn't know my innermost secrets since we grew up together in Brooklyn, and went to the same grammar school, high school and college. She has been my best friend since then and seems to be the only person who truly gets me. She understands me in ways that no one else ever will. She has been there for every single heartbreak, every silly decision that I made, and has never judged me. We have an unconditional respect and love for each other, which a lot of friends don't have in their friendship. We've never judged each other's decisions', or threw in each other's face if we made a truly bad one after advising each other against it. We just roll with it.

Darren is the father of my two oldest children. He moved out two years ago after living together for five years. He had to since I caught him cheating and after all these years I decided I wouldn't take it anymore. He didn't want to change and the relationship just seemed to be going around in circles. I honestly tried to make it work, but all the lies had finally caught up to him.

The woman I fell in love with was not my first experience, but she is my first RELATIONSHIP with another woman. This is where all the confusion starts. I've known her for many years. We were friends since high school, but I never knew she was gay and neither did she. Then again let me change that, she never admitted to herself that she was gay but according to her she was "watching" my ass since then. We went to college together and we always seemed to play this back and forth flirting game with each other. She dated my roommate in our first year at Howard University, and I must admit I was jealous of all the time and affection Zayle was giving my roommate. But hey, I am not attracted to women right? So why am I jealous?

Well I knew why I was jealous. Since our freshman year Zayle and I grew close. Studying together for our exams, going to parties together, even bunking in each other's rooms some times, but nothing ever happened between us. We would listen to each other's relationship problems. We even met each other's families since we both came from Brooklyn and would take turns driving to Brooklyn on holidays or whenever we just felt like taking a break from school. But she had one habit that always would cause us to malice each other. Whenever she hooked up with a new girl, it was forget all about Anaiyah until the girl either messed up or did something to piss her off.

One night, we all went to a sorority party and needless to say we were all DRUNK out of our minds. On the way back to our room I noticed Zayle trailing behind Andrea. Andrea and I had been roommates for about two semesters and although she claimed she wasn't gay or bi-sexual she always seemed to be half naked and flirting with Zayle every time we came back to the room together. I even confronted her once asking her straight to the point if she had ever been with a woman before. She seemed embarrassed but said that she had only kissed a girl before.

It was surprising to me when she and Zayle finally hooked up. It was even more surprising that it was happening regularly every other night and I would end up in the lounge on the couch. Now in my head I am thinking, ok they are not kicking my ass out tonight, so something has to give. I mean what the hell are they doing in there any damn way all freaking night?

So in my bed I hop and as you can imagine the room is only but so big. As soon as I lay across my bed all I could see was Andrea on her bed, legs wide open. "OK, hello people I am here...." was all I could think. Zayle doesn't seem to care since eating pussy is her thing and she has no shame. In her mind I am not even there. All I am hearing is some serious moaning and groaning, but I'm afraid to look, however after a while I couldn't help but to look. Curiosity got the best of me. I couldn't really see anything but the top of Zayle's head and Andrea's legs, but from the way Andrea was carrying on my imagination started to run wild.

About an hour later, yes I said an hour later, Andrea passes out. In between my half sleep and half listening, I feel someone standing over me stroking my face but I wasn't startled. Zayle always did that, always stroked my face, always tells me she loves me and always kisses my cheek. See, she is also my best friend, my ride or die.

8

I don't think there is anything we wouldn't do for each other to this very day. People always accused us of being together, but up until years later it wasn't true. So here she is standing over me and for the first time I looked up and saw a different Zayle. She looked attractive to me, even sexy. Now mind you she's not your typical girl. She's an AG, which stands for the aggressive female in the relationship who dresses like a boy and has aggressive mannerisms. She doesn't think she's a guy. She just dresses like one. She's always been that way since the day I met her in the 9th grade. That is one of the things that I loved and respected about her that she was true to herself even when no one else understood or accepted her, she always stayed true to herself. But here she is standing over me looking at me stroking my face and she leans over and says, "Can I ask u something?"

In my half sleep voice I say, "Yes."

"Did you get turned on? I saw you watching us," she asks.

All I could think is I am embarrassed and I am wondering why would she ask me something like this, not knowing that while I thought I was hiding the fact that I was turned on and playing with myself, she was watching me all along. I had my eyes closed, hell I figured she would be too busy and into what she was doing that she wouldn't notice me, or what I was doing. She stood over me just watching me, never touching me. I am dying for her to touch me. Instead all she did was stand there, pulling on her cigarette slowly.

"Anaiyah have you ever thought about being with me, ever?" She continued, "Nai, would you ever allow me to make love to you one day in this life time?"

I never answered her because she never allowed me to and I was glad. What was I to say?

Was I to say no even though that would have been a lie? Was I to admit that every time that we were together hanging out and she made a pass at someone else, I would wonder why not me? Wasn't she attracted to me, in any way at all? She bent over and kissed me on my cheek. Damn it, who knows what would have happened if only she had made a pass at me. I don't even know myself. That night was the last night that we were ever alone together. The following week we graduated and lost contact with each other.

During my residency in one of New York's finest hospitals I met Darren. He was tall, handsome, and swept me off my feet. He picked me up at the end of every shift being the perfect gentleman until he started to change slowly after the second year of our relationship. He started sleeping out, always using the excuse that he had to work except his paycheck never reflected all of this supposed overtime that he was working. Darren would leave for work at 5:30 am, and his shift was indeed supposed to finish at 4:30 in the afternoon. He worked with New York's Department of Sanitation, and had been there for twelve years. Due to seniority he was able to pull all of the overtime that was offered, which has been his excuse every night for about six months, until I got smart. I kept asking Darren, "Are you seeing someone yes or no?"

Of course he would never just say yes, it was always no. However, that didn't make sense since our sex life had now dwindled down to once every other week. This is from a man who would want sex at least every other night. Now suddenly he always had a headache and was too tired. His cell phone would go off at all hours of the night and he would always say it was his job. But seriously let's consider this... Why would his job call him several times back to back and then on top of it all text him at least ten times back to back? Let's be real!

One day, he accidentally punched in his cell phone code in front of me and I memorized it in my head for future use. He started coming home with new clothes in shopping bags, which was weird from a man who could not stand to go shopping at any time. When I would ask where these things came from, he would say that he went shopping. I would always reply "With whom?"

Ladies we have all at some point in time had that gut feeling that would not go away. This night I had that feeling. He called me and told me that he had to work overtime. It was already 10:30 p.m.

"What were you doing from 4:30 until now?" I asked.
"Wouldn't that be considered overtime already? You need to come home and help me with the girls." He started to offer an explanation and suddenly stopped. Something just didn't seem right.

"What kind of games are you playing Darren?" I asked him. "Yo, chill out and stop accusing me of shit." he screamed back and hung up. He always had a way of making me think that I was being un- reasonable and jumping to conclusions, even causing me to doubt my own intuitions. But I decided tonight I was going to follow my intuitions at all costs. I called Dahlia, "Dee, borrow your boyfriend's car and meet me around the corner from Darren's job."

" Why?" she questioned me.

"I'll explain later, just please trust me," I begged.

I took a cab there and met up with her. We sat and waited and about fifteen minutes later Darren came out, waved good-bye to his friends and hopped in his car never stopping to look around. Why would he?

As far as he was concerned, Anaiyah is a big fool and home in her bed. We drove behind him always keeping at least a car length away.

He was so busy on the phone that we drove behind him all the way from Brooklyn to Long Island and he never noticed us. We watched him pull up in front of a house, park the car and walk up to the door. I really wanted to see who would open the door except he used his own key. I was extremely happy that Dahlia dragged me to all of her yoga classes because I was seriously about to hop out of this car and kick his ass, but I had to use restraint. I had to get solid proof.

We sat there for hours contemplating different schemes of finding out who lived there. None of them seemed as if they would work. I called his cell phone to see if he would answer but he sent me to voice mail. I even texted him and told him that I had to take our daughter to the hospital, he never replied. I finally decided to just walk up and ring the bell. That's it, just like that. Three hours and many tears later, I walked up to the door and rang the bell. What happened next would destroy my life, as I knew it then. He came to the door and answered dressed in his boxers and a robe, rubbing his eyes as if I had disturbed him from a peaceful sleep. Before I had the chance to even slap the shit out of him, a woman appeared behind him, dressed only in a t-shirt, with a very pregnant belly protruding from underneath.
"Honey who is it at this time of night?" she asked. Before he could even turn to answer her, I spat straight in his face and pushed pass him.

"Who am I? Who are you? What the hell is going on?" I screamed frustratingly.

"Anaiyah get out! What are you doing here?" he started to yell at me. Is this man fucking crazy?

The woman then comes closer to me and says, "Oh your Anaiyah aren't you?"

See this to me just means that you know about me and it is now open season for me to whoop your ass.

"Well I'm Diana, and in case you're wondering yes this is Darren's baby!" she adds.

"His what? Bitch you must be out of your mind? Darren's what?" I didn't even finish my sentence before I swung at her catching the collar of her t-shirt. I dragged her into me and started to punch her. I lost my mind. I didn't care that she was pregnant or that I was on her property and that if she called the cops I was sure to be arrested. Dahlia raced in and grabbed me off of her, reminding me that I had a career to protect and two kids at home. "Nai these mother fuckers aren't worth it!" she pleaded. I let her go but not before knocking everything off of the table that was at the side of her door.

"Anaiyah you bitch! Get the fuck out of my house, I won't be pregnant for long bitch!" she promised.

"Darren, what the fuck do you have to say about all of this?" I asked this dumb motherfucker and as he stood there looking stupid.

"Yo, I didn't tell you to come over here! You or your home girl!" he smirked.

"EXCUSE ME? WHAT?" I screamed. I wanted to rush him to clothesline his ass but Dahlia grabbed me.

"Bitch I'm telling you I will call the police!" she said while rubbing her stomach.

"Darren would you really allow this bitch to call the police on me?" I asked him glaring him in his eyes. His actions gave me my answer. He turned around and walked away as if I wasn't even standing there.

He starts to yell and argue all this bullshit that I really didn't want to hear. All that was left for me to do was swallow my pride, leave and go home. As I turned around to walk away, I saw Long Island's finest approaching with no sirens just lights flashing. Dahlia and I looked at each other in shock and amazement. Did they really call the police?

"Darren? Did you really call the police?" I asked with tears streaming down my face; after all these years and on top of it all he was wrong. He was cheating on me and he had the nerve to call the police on me, or to even allow her to call them on me?

The officers approached.

"Hi is there a problem here?"

She stepped from behind Darren, "Yes officer these ladies are here harassing me?"

"Ladies is this true?" the officers ask. Darren just walked away as if he didn't know me. Oh my God.

"I.D. ladies? Does anyone have warrants or anything that I will find?"

As I reached into my wallet to hand him my license, Dahlia had already given him hers. I tried to explain to him, "Officer, this is my man and he is here cheating on me with this woman. I didn't come here for her, I came here for him." He looked me straight in the eye, and had a slight smirk on his face that really pissed me off, but what was I to say?

They took our IDs and ran them. There were no warrants or anything.

They walked back to us "Ladies regardless of what is going on, it is our duty to escort you off of the property." With all this going on Darren didn't even stand at the door to see what was going on and he never even came back or spoke to the officers. Thank God they just told us to leave the property. They walked us back to our car, and drove behind us for a block or two to make sure we really left. Dahlia drove as I cried all the way home. As soon as I got there I packed every single piece of his belongings and had Dahlia's man drop them off at the house that we followed him to. I then called the locksmith and had every single lock changed. Afterwards I changed my cell phone and house phone numbers.

I was so out of it the next morning I called my doctor and got a sick note for work. There was no way that I was going to be able to function at work. How could I? I can't believe that this asshole got over on me. This is ridiculous. While I sit there running everything through my mind over and over, Darren shows up ringing my doorbell off the hook.

"Darren get the hell away from my fucking door. There is nothing at all for us to discuss." I scream at him. Then I remember... I opened the door, "As a matter of fact give me my fucking bank card right now".

"Anaiyah that bitch lied to you! That is not my baby!" he tried to explain.

"Ok that is not your baby but the funny thing is you didn't say shit when you were standing in front of her right? Do you think I'm a fool?" I exclaimed. "And wait a minute, are we forgetting the fact that you were laid up in the bitch house like you live there?"

Then it dawned on me, "I can't believe we are even standing here having this damn discussion. What is there to talk about? I saw the shit with my own eyes, it's not like anyone told me. You know what Darren; you stay here with the kids. I need some time for myself." I walked out and went straight to Dahlia's house. I didn't even take a change of clothes.

Thank God she had given me an extra key. I didn't know where she was but I just needed some time to think. Just a few hours for myself was all I needed. I started to think, "How could I have been so stupid? How did he get over on me? I was trying my best to be the perfect "wifey". Where did I go wrong?" I sacrificed even my friends, putting all my energy and time into him. I did everything I thought a "wifey" was supposed to do. Pushing him forward, encouraging him to go back to school and get a college degree, not knowing that I was making him a better man for another woman and a better father for someone else's child. I block my number and call his phone. Straight to voice mail...BINGO that's exactly what I wanted. I punched in his code and Presto... "You have 2 new voicemails, Message number one from 631-555-9087: 'Hey Darren when are you coming back home? Its time you quit playing this game, bring all your stuff tonight or else.'

WOW.

Ok how am I going to deal with this? I decided to give her trifling ass a call. I dial her number back first blocked but she didn't answer. Then I figure, why the hell am I blocking my number, I'm a grown ass woman and she is with my man, well he's supposed to be my man, so why am I hiding? I un- block my cell phone number and call her back.

"Hello?" she answers.

"Hello, this is Anaiyah. I need to know exactly what is going on with you and Darren?"

"Listen Anaiyah, you saw for yourself what is going on with me and Darren. What would you like me to tell you, my due date?"

Wait a damn minute this heifer must have lost her mind? I see I'm gonna have to take it back to the days of when I just didn't give a fuck.

"Listen, whatever your name is, because I really don't care, but do you take me for a joke? How long have you and he been together?" I asked.

She starts to laugh. "Well missy, long enough for me to be pregnant, how 'bout that?"
"Well he denies that the baby is his." I thought that would pierce her soul since she wanted to be cocky about the whole shit.

"Really Miss Anaiyah, well that's fine because that is what DNA tests are for, right?" she asks sarcastically.

Before I could respond, she continued. "Do me a favor, don't call my number back, ok? Take this shit up with your man. Oh yeah and by the way, I will be hitting the both of you up for child support."

I had to laugh because that statement immediately stopped my tears. "Good luck on that one bitch, he barely can take care of himself and we're not married, if you thought you would be getting any of my money!" With that she hung up on me.

I contemplated calling her back, but had to stop and think, who am I really hurting? Not her because she already knew about me. I was only hurting myself.

I called him though. This time he picked up.

"Darren I just spoke to your bitch and just to let you know she is taking your ass to child support court, you fucking bastard. You're a liar."

"Anaiyah that is not my child, please stop your shit.", he pleads.

In the middle of us arguing, she calls me back. "Really, so why is she beeping in on the other line huh?" I asked.

"You know what Anaiyah, you and her can both go to hell!" Now isn't this a bitch he has an attitude as if I did something to him. I didn't even bother to answer her and she didn't leave a voice mail either. Dahlia's house was nice and peaceful but I decided to leave before she came home. I didn't want to get into it with her.

She knew everything that he ever did to me and couldn't understand why the hell I was still there and to be honest, I didn't know why either.

I guess part of it was that I was just use to him. I never really dated anyone else. I don't know how to date. It's not that I wasn't asked out on dates, I just couldn't deal with the getting to know someone else part, plus I had the girls and my career. I didn't have time to figure out someone new. I didn't want to confuse the girls. They didn't deserve that. I saw my friends dating and even got a little jealous at times, but I just didn't want to expose my girls to a new *"friend"* every few months. My parents were stable and married for forty years, and I wanted the same stability for my girls.

Darren and I were together for a total of eight years. We always spoke about marriage and getting engaged but never took it any further.

He never produced a ring, never formally proposed, but somehow every time we got into a big argument that would threaten our relationship he would suggest marriage. He even convinced me once that he was serious and ready so I started to actually plan the "wedding". I went as far as choosing my bridesmaids and maid of honor. We went to look at places, sampled food, priced DJ's… everything! I told my entire family and all of my friends. Everyone said the same thing, "Anaiyah, are you sure he is not just leading you on to keep you quiet? How is he planning to marry you? You don't even have a ring?"

That was a serious factor, "Where was my ring?" I asked him. I even brought up the fact that I looked like a delusional bride trying on all these different wedding gowns with no engagement ring on my finger. I was embarrassed but I always played it off each time someone would ask to see my ring explaining that in my field of work I washed and banged my hands too frequently to keep on a diamond ring. He even went as far as to produce a ring box once in the middle of one of our heated arguments stating that the ring was in that box and if I didn't "behave" I would never see it.

After that argument I searched in vain every single time he left searching for the ring and never finding it or the box. That led me to believe that it was an empty box all along. His excuse for not ever giving me a ring was that I needed to *earn it*. EARN IT? Imagine that. This from a man that I put up with all of his bullshit lies, telling me that I needed to earn it!

He complained that I never had enough time for him, and I would always have to defend the fact that I was trying to advance in my medical career to secure a future for the kids and for him. In my heart I knew he was full of shit but I never wanted to admit it, especially to everyone else. He played it off well although participating in everything that I wanted him to. Just to later find out he had another woman pregnant.

I wanted to establish my career before committing myself to a marriage and the girls came along unexpectedly. Saniyah, my oldest girl, is seven years old. She looks like me and has her father's outgoing and hilarious spirit. She could make anyone smile on his or her worse day. She was the one that would come in and tell you to smile and that everything would be ok. She loved school and loved to read. Darren would come in every night and read a story to her religiously.

Yael is four years old going on forty. She was the fire spirit in the house. She was more like me but looked like her father. She would argue and debate her point until the person she was in the debate with would just give up. She would enter the room with such confidence and make her statement. I would feel sorry for Saniyah when they would go at it over whose turn it was to use the computer. Yael would have the dates and times of each time Saniyah logged on down to the web sites. We loved them dearly and wanted to make a family for them. So what happened?

I know that my schooling and career took up a lot of time, but wouldn't a man want that? Wouldn't a real man want a woman with an education and a career that was trying to better herself. At times like this, I would say no. For now, I have to get myself into a private practice or a hospital. I need a stable income, and to get all of my school bills under control before I can put him out of our lives completely.

I hope I can mentally survive this.

Chapter 2

ive years later I'm sitting in the library studying for my interview with a prestigious uptown practice. I'm nervous, I'm tired and I'm stressed out. How am I going to pass this exam? How am I going to get through this interview? I'm working at a full time job in a pediatric office that is driving me insane. I'm working long hours, getting home late, studying late and having relationship problems, not to mention money problems.

I walk into the library-soaking wet because it's pouring rain outside and as usual I didn't listen to the weather report so I am unprepared. I walk in flustered and feeling extremely miserable so I sit down and put my head on the table. My test is two days away. Will I be ready is all that is going through my head. Should I even bother? Should I put off the interview and reschedule? I'm in the midst of my thoughts and I feel someone staring at me. Now who the hell is staring at me looking a mess. I really don't want to look up but I am curious. My baseball cap is blocking my vision, but I glance up from under the brim and I see a set of hands in front of me offering me a cup of coffee. Oh my God!!! It's Zayle!!
I jump up, "Where have you been?"

"Well I'm here researching a case that I'm getting ready to try in criminal court. I just went to get this cup of coffee, but you look like you need it more than I do." I didn't know if that was a compliment but I was more than happy to accept. She took a seat in front of me and we started to study separately. Seven hours later and I had enough. My eyes were dry and blurry from reading so much. "Hey I'm leaving... I've had enough."

"Wait for me. I was just about to wrap it up!" We gathered our things and left. On our way to the parking lot the rain held up and she walked me to my car.

When she saw my jeep she had a look of amazement. I drove the exact same Mercedes Benz jeep, same model and year as hers.

She started to laugh and said "Wow, you're a woman with class," and explained why she was laughing. After ten minutes of us just standing there she asked, "Hey would you like to go get something to eat? I know this new restaurant not too far away from here."

I was feeling hungry so why not? She went and got her jeep and I followed behind her. All the way there I am trying to fix myself up. I let out my hair, put on some lip-gloss and sprayed on my favorite perfume *"BOND NO 9"*. Remember I haven't seen her since that night back in the dorm room when she and Andrea were getting it on. We drove a few miles and drove into the valet parking area. Thank God my *"Gucci"* heels were in the back of my jeep.

We stepped into the restaurant and the Maitre D seated us. She walked in front of me and pulled out my chair, waited for me to take my seat and pushed my chair in. Wow, I am a little impressed. She remembered that I didn't drink but suggested that I have a glass of wine. She asked the waiter for the wine list and ordered me a glass of Chardonnay and an apple martini for herself. We sipped and chatted until the food came. It was so unreal as though no time had passed between us at all. We spoke about everything; everything that we could possibly think of. We laughed, we even vented about our current relationship problems, and it seemed so natural, so comfortable.

In the middle of the conversation we remembered we didn't have each other's current phone numbers and reached onto our hips and pulled out the exact same phones. Ok is this destiny or coincidence? We ate our dinners and desserts and I reached over and fed her a piece of my Chocolate Mousse cake. To my surprise I noticed how beautiful her eyes were. Funny enough, I never noticed that before. At the same moment that I noticed her eyes she commented on how beautiful my eyes and lips were. The scary thing is I was admiring her eyes and lips in my head. Except I would never voice that, what would she think?

The waiter asked if we were finished and ready for the bill. I was finished but wasn't ready to go home, but she said yes and he brought the bill. As he approached us with the bill I reached in to my pocket book for my wallet to get my credit card. She looked at me as if I was crazy. "Girl put that back into your bag!" See that was a force of habit since I was so used to paying for dinners even if I was invited. We exited the restaurant and the valet brought our jeeps to us. "Just pull out of the parking lot and wait," she demanded. So I did as she asked.

She pulled in front of my jeep and walked back to my car. I got out to meet her but as she walked up to meet me, I noticed how nicely she was dressed and that she had a sexy walk. Ok wait a minute, did I just say that a WOMAN had a sexy walk. Now I get nervous. Am I drunk from one glass of wine? What is going on with me? I've never been attracted to a woman. I've had my encounters but it was always just sexual, but here I am "attracted". Maybe the difference was that she was a "dyke", a female that dresses like a guy. The thing is she just looks natural, not as if she is trying to be a dude or look like one. For all the years I have known her this is just her. Could that be it? She approaches me and I find myself nervous. Is my hair fixed? My lip-gloss on? My clothes fixed? Do I still smell good?

"What's going on?", I asked.

"Do you have to go straight home? If you want to hang I know this poetry club over in Manhattan."

"Sure!" I said excitedly. Why not? I had nothing else to do and no one to go home to. She tells me to follow behind her. As I turn to get into my car, she turns and grabs my hand and tells me to stay behind her and that she would not drive fast. We hop into our jeeps and pull off. I start to blast my music. We drive on and I make sure I keep up. As we were approaching the bridge she calls me "Are you ok?"

"Yes I am fine."

All the while I'm thinking to myself "Ok... What's all this about?" but I am enjoying this. She calls me to tell me to exit on the FDR. As we exit she says to "Stay to the left. It's right off the first exit."

As we're exiting she calls me again. This time she says, "Pull over." I'm wondering what is wrong. We pull over and she walks up to my window but her face looks serious; I'm wondering what's wrong? She starts to apologize profusely that her girlfriend just called her and that she needs to go home.

"It's ok! Don't worry about it, I completely understand." Now why would I be upset? It wasn't a date. We were just hanging out.

"I'm not upset! Call me in the morning." I assured her. She gives me a hug and I jumped into my car, made a U turn and head on home.

Yes I was disappointed, but really and truly for what? It's not like we had planned a date. Date?

Ok did I just think Date?

Chapter 3

I really didn't have to look at the caller ID because I already knew who it was. All I heard on the other end was "Girl get dressed, I'll be there in 30 minutes," click in my ears. I jumped in the shower, washed my hair, pumped the music and started to get dressed. I threw on a simple black dress, well at least it was simple in the front but there was no back and the cut went all the way down to the crack off my ass. I threw on my Gucci stilettos, sprayed on my signature fragrance "*Bond NO. 9, Noho Nuit,*" and then the doorbell rang. Dahlia screaming "Come on girl let's go! Who's driving?"

I told her, "You drive! I'm drinking tonight." I had to laugh at the expression that came over her face. She looked at me stunned with her mouth open.

"DRINKING? Ok you have to tell me what happened with Zaye?"

"Girl please, we'll talk about that later. Let's go!"

I deliberately left my car keys on the kitchen table, slammed my door and ran to the passenger side of her Jeep. I hope we're not going to the city because I really felt like staying local.

Of course she had a fit but since she chose the club the last time what I want goes. Thank GOD because I was really tired and just felt like hearing music. It was packed by the time we got there. We finally found a park and after waiting about 15 minutes in the line we entered the club. We walk in and the club is packed to the brim.
The crowd is jumping, the music is pumping, and it's so crowded we can't even make our way to the bar. Now Dee

knows how I feel about walking through crowds so I confidently find a corner and take my stance. She goes to the bar and comes back with water for me, "Bitch, I said I was drinking tonight!" I kindly sent her back to the bar.

As she returned from the bar with my apple martini with the salted rim, just the way I like it, this sweaty guy, looking like he just came out the gym, approaches me. If he had gotten any closer he would've kissed me. "Hey beautiful you want to dance?" Now I'm annoyed he is invading my personal space and instead of Dahlia rescuing me, she's standing there laughing at me. I'm looking at her like ok I am going to get you. Then I feel someone place their hand on my lower back, and before I could turn around to slap the shit out of the person I hear, "Don't turn around sexy, it's me."

"Me who?" I ask curiously.

I turn around and it's Zayle. "Oh shit! Hey babe what are you doing here?" She comes in front of me and gives me a big hug.

"I'm here with my girl. One of her friends is celebrating their birthday," she explains.

"Oh ok, I just didn't know that you go to straight clubs?"

She looked at me like I was crazy, and asked me "Why not?" I didn't know how to answer that question. I did notice that she looked very, very nice and showed her Dahlia who was standing with her back turned. I went to Dahlia and said, "Look who's here?"

Dahlia loudly screams, "ZAY!! WHAT'S UP?" and jumps on her. We all start to laugh and as I look over Zaye's back I notice a female slowly approaching.

She kissed Zayle on her neck as if to show possession. In my head I'm saying sweetie don't worry I'm straight. Zayle introduced us as her friends since high school and college. We smiled and exchanged handshakes. We all ended up partying the night away, me throwing back martinis as if it were water and Dahlia drinking water because tonight she was the designated driver. HAHA…

At about 4 a.m., I decided that my body couldn't take any more liquor. "Zaye I'm leaving. The next time your single let me know," I whispered and leaned in to kiss her on her cheek.

What the hell did I just say? Ok it's really time to go because the martinis are talking. To my surprise she whispered back, "Why wait till then?" If I could describe the look that came over my face it still wouldn't do any justice.
All the way home, I am wondering what the hell came over me? Dahlia is yapping in my ear but I didn't hear a single word she was saying. I'm too busy concentrating on what just transpired. Why the hell did I just say that? What the hell was I thinking? Am I crazy? Nah I'm drunk that's it. That is the only explanation.

We pull up into my driveway; I hop out the car and kiss her good night. I run into the house and as I'm closing my door I hear "Call Me!" I'm in the house short of thirty minutes. I kick my shoes off, turn my music on and light my candles. I'm wondering if I'm going to burn the house down, but hey how often am I relaxed? All of a sudden I hear a knock at my door.

"Dahlia, go home! You're not drunk!" I'm saying as I open the door. Only it's not Dahlia its Zayle "Oh shit!"

She must have seen the shock on my face because she asked me, "Do you have company? Is it a bad time?"

"No, I'm home alone." As soon as I got the last words out of my mouth she pulls her hand from behind her with two dozen of the most beautiful fire and ice long stemmed roses I had ever seen in my life. She handed them to me and before I could say anything she turns to walk out of the door. I grab her hand to stop her. I turn her around and she says, "The roses are to apologize for leaving you earlier."

I tell her that it's ok, hug her and tell her how beautiful the roses were. As I went to kiss her on her cheek, our lips brushed and we started to kiss. It was the most passionate kiss I had ever felt in my life and my knees got weak. But I couldn't let her know! How is this possible? This is a woman why am I getting wet? What are these feelings that I am having? Is it because it's Zayle, and I've always wondered what it would feel like to have her kiss me, passionately, the way I've seen her kiss all of her girlfriends over the years.

It felt as if we were kissing forever but I couldn't stop her and I didn't want to. We ended up kissing and backing up into my kitchen. Where is all this passion coming from? Could it be because I haven't slept with a soul besides my own hands since Darren left? She quickly turned me around and started tracing my tattoos down my back with her fingers. My body started to tremble. She turned me around and started to caress my legs. I found myself opening my legs slightly, with hesitation, but they were still opening. She started to kiss my legs all the way up to my inner thigh and then she stopped to come up to my ear and whispered to me, "Do you want me to stop?"

HELL NO! I screamed in my head but managed to whisper "No." But was I sure?

I don't know why, but my legs wouldn't close and I wouldn't say no. My body wouldn't say no.

She whispered "Ok," and started to kiss me again. My legs flew around her and somehow, I don't even know why, but I couldn't let her go. She took her time, caressing me while unwrapping my legs from around her. She whispered, "I've wanted this for years," and went back to kissing my legs. The closer she got to my pussy the wetter I got. My body trembled with anticipation. This I wasn't use to. First of all, I've had to use lubricants for years and the second issue was that this is Zaye from high school, college, and a female. But tonight there was no need for lubricants. The next thing I felt was something warm parting my lips, not the set on face, but the set between my legs.

"OH MY GOD!!" That's all I could scream in my head. She made love to my pussy with her tongue in a way that I've never felt before. I couldn't think straight. I thought I was going to break her neck the way my body kept jumping and jerking off of the table. To make it worse it was as if she was teasing me. When I couldn't take it anymore I grabbed her head and practically tried to shove it into my pussy. In my head I'm thinking ok wait turn back. It was too late before I could even think to say stop. My body exploded in the most intense orgasm I had ever felt in my entire life. She eases up to me kisses me passionately and tells me "It's sweeter than I ever imagined, but I have to go."

What the fuck? Is she for real? She gets up, wipes her mouth with her handkerchief, and walks over to my door. She looks back and sees me sprawled out on the table, pussy still wet.

"Go ahead, I'll lock it later," I say, and she leaves.

Did this really just happen?

Did a female really eat me out and leave?

.

A man has never done that to me and a woman just did. Hell no this shit is crazy.

Is this the beginning or the end?

Chapter 4

It seemed that as soon as I closed my eyes the sun rose. Oh God, I'm tired and my body hurts. I have a hangover that feels like someone is literally slamming my head between two doors. Why the hell did I drink so much was the first thought that came to my head. The second was where the hell was my cell phone? I reached over and grabbed it to see ten missed calls and five text messages. Who the hell could this be from? My initial thought was Dahlia because the girl doesn't sleep. She seems to run on solar energy. I've never seen anyone like her before. To my surprise it was Zayle. Immediately, I got flash backs from the night before.

Her texts went like this:

1- Hey morning
2- I'm sorry I left like that, r u up?
3- Listen if ur mad at me can u pls jst ans me so ill know and stop texting u.
4- Ok, I can understand if ur upset but pls let me explain face to face.
5- Anaiyah pls ans me, I'm sorry.

I got up and called my mom to check on the kids since they were spending the weekend at her house. As soon as I was about to shut down my phone Zayle beeped in so I clicked over. "Hey morning, I just got your texts."

"Listen I need to see you please, I need to explain to you what happened and why I left like that," she pleaded.

"Zaye, it's no problem. I really understand," which was a lie, but does it really matter at this point. I agreed to meet up with her at her house and quickly jotted down the directions. I got up, took a shower, straightened up the house a bit and left. All the way there I am thinking why am I going there? She really doesn't owe me an explanation.

What happened, happened, just let it be. I've known Zaye for years and although we never slept together, we've always flirted but from a distance. Which maybe was a safer choice and I just didn't know. When I say safer, I mean safer on my heart, our hearts.

I pull up and walk to her door. She was already standing there when I raised my hand to knock at the door. I almost knocked on her face how suddenly the door opened. The first thing I noticed was how cute she looked and how nice and neat her place was. It smelled fresh and was well decorated.
Then I noticed feminine clothes, which definitely were not hers. I didn't mention it. I just let it go. I didn't want to appear nosey. As I took a seat I gazed around and noticed pictures of them up around the house. "Beautiful pictures," I commented just to let her know that yes, I see them. I'm not blind. She ignored my comment and offered me a beverage. I kindly took my glass and we sat down to talk. The first thing out of her was "I'm sorry."

"Sorry for what?" I asked her. "Are you sorry that you ate me out and left me right there? What are you sorry for?" This I had to hear. She comes and sits so close to me that I could smell her shampoo that she used in her hair. Now I'm pissed, aren't I? Why am I feeling vulnerable? These are the questions that I am asking in my head.

She moves closer, takes my hand, takes a deep breath, and says, "Here it goes. I feel really bad about this morning. Not about us, not about what happened, but just the fact that you're with someone, and so am I." She continued, "We're both in relationships and to make it worse I don't sleep with straight women or bi-sexual women, so I can't even explain why I did what I did."

34

I tried to respond but she continued, "Maybe it is the fact that for all these years I've been attracted to you and finally got a chance. But I don't want it to ruin our friendship."

Wow, with all that I replied, "Ok."

What was I to say? She was honest and she was right. We were both in separate relationships, living two different lives, happy or not the "others", as I would refer to our "significant others", didn't deserve that.

"I've been out living the gay lifestyle for years and I've been accepted by my family and friends. Going back to hiding and sneaking around was not an option," she explained. "I can't afford to fall in love with you and risk my heart being broken."

I had nothing to say. I wasn't prepared to respond to something so deep that I'd never thought of before. She was right. Was I ready to fall in love with a woman, and let the whole world know?

We sat there for a few more hours, just talking about everything that we were going through in our lives. Right now we were both going through difficult relationships. I lay in her lap as she told me about her girlfriend. She told me that they had been together since she was in law school. That they met in a club and she wasn't attracted to her physically at first but that she really stuck by her while she went to school, even supported her monetarily when shit was tight.
In a way she felt obligated to her. She found out two years ago that she was a drug addict and she was hooked to prescription drugs.

She felt somewhat a sense of guilt that maybe all those hard times they went through with money while she was in law school is what drove her to start getting high.

"The worst part of it all is that Suzanne's family blames me". I signed her up for a drug program, but after two weeks she signed herself out. I don't know what else to do," she explains.

"Don't blame yourself. Even if things were hard, you never put the pills in her hands and you actually tried to help her get better. Don't place the blame on yourself." I just wanted to relieve her sense of guilt.

I told her about Darren and his cheating ways and that I caught him in the other woman's house. "The woman actually came out and told me that she was indeed pregnant by him." She sat there in shock. "Don't feel sorry for me. It's ok. I did what I had to do and put his ass out. It wasn't as if he didn't have somewhere to go. After a lot of investigative work on my behalf, I found out that after all the years that he was crying "broke"; the house that I went to in Long Island was actually his house. Imagine that? That is why he never had money to do anything in our house or pay any bills. At first I didn't believe it until my girlfriend, who is into real estate, actually got me proof in black and white." There it was Darren Walker was the sole owner of the property. To make it worse, I never knew about it and he let another woman live in it while the girls and I lived in a three-bedroom apartment.

"The only time that he is at my house now, is when I have to work late and the girls have to go to school, which was very seldom anyway because my mother usually had the children for me." I continued to explain. After talking for a while, we decided to go get some food and have a drink.

We decided to go to Bay Ridge and get some seafood. All the way there we just relaxed and played some music.

"Nai, I am so glad that you didn't change. You are the same Anaiyah Williams that I always loved."

"Same here Zaye, same here."

We got to the restaurant. We were seated and immediately our orders were taken. I was impressed by the fast service here.

"Nai, I've heard an old wives tale that raw clams make you horny." She burst out into laughter.

"Wouldn't you like to know?"

We ate our food and left the restaurant. I asked her to drive back because I really didn't like to drive, unless I really had to. I would just about let anyone drive as long as they had a license.

"Nai, you know I enjoyed you last night right?" She continued. "I didn't want to stop, trust me. I've wanted you for years. You tasted so fucking good, but I don't do bi-sexual women." She started to laugh at me.

"Bi-sexual? Right now trust me, I'm not fucking anyone and I enjoyed it too." I started to blush.

"Why are you blushing?" She had this way of asking me questions in a way that made me nervous.

"I'm not blushing, am I?" I looked in the mirror and I was as red as if someone had slapped me dead square in my face. We pulled up into her driveway, which was a great save for me, because now I wouldn't have to answer her.

"Thanks for a great evening babe," I leaned in and gave her a hug and a kiss.

"Thank you too baby, call me later ok."

I drove off and went home.

As soon as I pushed the key in my door I knew something was wrong. My lights were on, and dishes were in my sink. Darren, was in my house.

"Hi, where are the girls?" I asked

"There sleeping in their room," he said while looking me up and down.

As soon as I opened my bedroom door I could see that he had been lying in my bed. My sheets were half off of the bed, the comforter was on the floor, and to make shit worse dishes were on my carpet.

"Darren how many times do I have to tell you, that when you come to watch the girls, I don't want you in my room at all! There is no reason for you to be in my room Darren, shit!" He just totally ignored me and went and plopped his ass in my bed. I didn't feel like arguing so I just went into the living room. Imagine, I have to be uncomfortable in my own home.

My cell goes off.
    Z- Hey babe what r u doing?
    Me- Hey, I'm home & Darren is here annoying me
    Z-   Same here Suzanne is high and breaking shit up
    Me- R u serious? I wish I could leave
    Z- U know what, fuck this bull shit, I want to make love to u, I want to make up for last night, will u let me
    Me- huh?

Z- Nai. U read my text.

Me- So I should let u make love to me so u can walk out on me again?

Z- Let me prove u wrong. Meet me at the Marriot, downtown Brooklyn 20 minutes.

Me- ok

I started flicking the channels on the T.V. looking for a "*Law and Order*" episode to watch. I am not going anywhere; she just fucking played me last night.

"Yo Anaiyah, why the hell didn't you sort out my clothes for me so that I could wash them. You knew I left some dirty clothes here."

"What? Do I look like your fucking maid? Let your pregnant bitch in Long Island wash them for you!"

That was it. I am going to the hotel. I am not going to stay here and argue with this asshole tonight. It had been already ten minutes since we text so I had ten minutes to get there. I decided to text her; I didn't want him eaves dropping on my conversation with her.

Me- babe I will b about 15 mins late ok, but I am cming

Z- ok babe, listen can I ask u something?

Me- Sure

Z- I know u slept with a woman b 4 but did u ever use a dildo?

Me-Yes, but I didn't like it

Z- u want to try it again, I always said u looked like u could ride a dick, lol

Lol meant laughing out loud.

Me- Z u r so nasty, yeah bring it y not. lol

I jumped in the shower. I made sure to douche because I wanted to smell as fresh as I possibly could. I couldn't believe that I was really leaving my house to go and have sex with Zayle. Boy oh Boy wait until Dahlia hears this one. She is going to have a field day asking me questions.

I jump in the car and make my way to Flatbush. I take it all the way straight to the hotel. I told Darren that I had to go by Dahlia for something and then I made sure to text and call her to tell her not to answer her phone, unless she saw my number. She agreed but of course she kept asking me, where was I going and with whom. I had to keep telling her I would tell her tomorrow. I pull up and texted Zaye:
Me-babe where r u?

She scared the living daylights out of me because she was standing right beside my car and I didn't see her. I jumped out of the jeep and she gave the valet my car keys. She noticed that I had a bag with me and asked me what was in it. I told her to mind her damn business. I had a few tricks up my sleeve for her. In my bag, I had a bustier that I had purchased from *"Fredrick's of Hollywood"* the week before to wear to a party that I never ended up going to. I threw in a tube of red *"Mac"* lipstick, I figured hey; since this will be our first and last time, why not make it memorable. We get the room key and head upstairs.

The room was lovely. A little chilly but really nice, I was impressed that she didn't offer to go to a motel. I must admit I was feeling a little nervous. If someone were to ask me right now exactly what was making me nervous, I wouldn't be able to pin point exactly what it was; maybe the fact that I made a conscious decision to have sex with her tonight. There was no way that I could blame liquor.

I immediately went into the bathroom once we got into the suite. I told her I would be right back. She told me it was fine because she was going to smoke a blunt anyway. I took off my clothes and decided to try to get into this contraption. God must have been on my side because I swear I almost hung myself trying to get into it. It was black Jacquard that laced completely in the back with a garter belt attachment to it. After nearly hanging myself I almost choked myself trying to pull the lace tight and tie it.

She must have been wondering what the hell I was doing in there but I still had to get the stockings on. After what seemed like eternity I finally got myself together. What was I going through all of this for anyway? This was a definite planned one-night stand. After tonight, I'm not sleeping with her again anyway. But I plan to make the best of it tonight so that she will always remember me.

I come out of the room, and I am feeling so nervous, thank God I didn't put any heels on. I surely would have busted my ass and that would not have been cute. There she was laying up on the bed in a black wife beater and black boxers. She was looking as cute as ever. At least for tonight I am willing to admit, that yes I am attracted to Zayle. The same Zayle from high school... I slowly walk over to the bed. All of my plans of walking over to the bed seductively went right out of the window. I could not believe that I was so nervous. The crazy thing is if she were a man, I would not have been nervous at all. I would have walked right out there as if I were a *"Victoria's Secret"* Model. Tyra Banks would have had nothing on me. When I get to her, I boldly straddle her as if I wanted to take control. In my head I really wanted her to take control but she seemed relaxed and comfortable with me taking control.

"Hey, are you ok? You seem nervous?" she asked.

I didn't even answer; I just started to kiss her. I was shocked it felt so fucking good. She took her hands and started to caress my body. It felt good except the damn corset was starting to feel uncomfortable now, the bone in the corset was starting to irritate the hell out of me. I felt like I couldn't breathe but I couldn't say that, I had to stay in character.

"Put it in," I leaned over and whispered in her ear.

She whispered back "No, babe, you put it in when you are ready."

Ok now all of these questions start going through my head, will it feel good? How can it possibly feel good, it's not real. My one and only experience with a strap on was nothing to write home about. I was annoyed and it hurt not to mention it did not feel good. I grabbed it and placed it in me. I closed my eyes and started to move on it. It hurt going in, since Darren and I had not had sex since I busted him with his woman in Long island.

She spoke to me the entire time, making sure that I was ok, I guess my face was showing that I was feeling a little pain, but not enough to make me stop.

"I love you. I've wanted you for all these years," she kept telling me. Did she mean it? She loved me? Maybe it was just the usual sex talk that guys give you when they're in bed with you, to make you feel like you're special; that the moment was special, after all she does think like a guy. But something was different, when she said "I love you", she looked me straight in my eyes and I couldn't look away. I then flipped her over so that she could be on top of me. What happened next shocked the shit out of me.

She moved so natural. I swear I closed my eyes and forgot that she was a woman. She didn't pump away, how some men pump away as if they are trying to go straight through to your back, but it was exactly how I liked it. The night ended with her going down on me for an hour and half. I had to ask her if her jaw wasn't hurting her.

"Hell no Nai! I've been waiting to make love to you for too many years and I'm going to enjoy every single minute. When I was at your house I played myself."

I just smiled. I had seven orgasms, and my damn knees were weak. We got dressed, and headed our separate ways. I just hugged her and told her that I would call her later that day, no long conversations. Just "Talk to you later."

I walked out, the same way that she walked out on me the night before. Except now I couldn't stop thinking about her. Fuck it what am I worried about? She did it to me right? I continued walking towards the elevator, never stopping to look back, just in case she was looking through the peephole. I couldn't let her see that I was affected. I had to keep my cool. I got down stairs to my car, climbed in and just started to cry. I wasn't exactly sure why I was crying but a sudden sea of emotions just came over me, and I just had the urge to cry. I dialed her number. No answer. I didn't leave a message, instead I texted her, and asked her to give me a call when she got the message.

With that I headed home.

Chapter 5

The entire ride home I was in shock at what just happened. I kept replaying the entire night over and over in my head and I was shocked at Zayle and myself. I reach for my cell phone and dial Dahlia. "Hello?" she sounded as if she was asleep, but I knew once I told her where I was coming from; she would suddenly be wide-awake.

"Dee, guess where I am coming from?"

"Anaiyah, it better be somewhere good, if you're waking me out of my sleep at 4a.m.,"she replied.

"Oh yes it is, trust me, I am coming from the *Marriot*."

"The *Marriott*? With who?" sounding as though she was beginning to fully wake up. I started to laugh, partly because I was embarrassed and partly because I still couldn't believe it.

"Zayle," I replied quickly waiting for the other end to explode.

"WHO? It sounded as if you said Zayle!"

"Yes, Dahlia, Zayle!"

"Are you serious and how the hell did that happen?" she asked. Before I could begin to answer her my phone beeped in and it was Darren. I told Dahlia that I would call her back and clicked over.

"Where the hell are you at this time of the morning? I need to leave to go to work!" I hung up on him because I didn't feel like arguing. I just had a good evening and didn't want to ruin it arguing with a man who was living his own life. I am sure he had to leave because his girlfriend called him for some kind of midnight craving. I was doing everything since that night to hold off from doing something stupid to him because, he wasn't worth it. I have two little girls to worry about and take care of but I am hurting badly. In the years that we had been together I never cheated on him; not even once. Needless to say now I see why he always accused me of cheating on him.

What happened tonight with Zayle; I wouldn't consider cheating because I threw him out, so technically I am single whether he wants to accept it or not. I drove as slowly as I could, making sure to let every red light catch me. The phone rings and it was Zayle.

"Hey babe, did you reach in your house as yet?"

"Hey Zayle, no not as yet, but can I call you back later in the morning?" She hesitated, almost sounding shocked that I didn't want to speak to her.

"Sure, you do that, lata", and hung the phone up very abruptly. It wasn't that I didn't want to speak to her, it was just that I was suddenly feeling very confused. Not about sleeping with her, because I made a conscious decision to do that. The confusion was why did I enjoy it so much? What was going to happen now? What if I wanted to sleep with her again? I reach my house and all of these thoughts now had to stop. I had all day tomorrow to try to figure this out.

I walk into the house and it as if he was just waiting for me to enter the house.

"Where the fuck are you coming from?" It was a good thing that I left the bag with my corset in the back of the truck. I didn't expect him to be up, and especially not waiting for me in the living room.

"Excuse me? Are you really questioning me? This from a man who has a woman pregnant by him?"

I stepped around him and headed for the bedroom. I just wanted to go to sleep and relish on what just happened. I put my cell phone on vibrate and stuck it in my end table drawer just in case she decided to call or text me back. I didn't want him in my business. He walks in and is still yelling at the top of his voice.

"Darren, shut the hell up! You are going to wake up the kids!" I scream back.

"You know what, I am not helping you with the fucking rent anymore! Let your new man help you!"

"Darren, you were always looking for an excuse, so go ahead! It won't faze me. Shut the door on your way out please, thank you!" I said uncaringly. I was tired of his shit and I had too much on my mind anyway. He walked out slamming every single door between the bedroom and the front door. It was amazing that the children didn't wake up. I got up and looked out the window just to make sure that he really left, went back to my room and took out my cell phone to call Zayle. What was I going to say? It was already 5 a.m. Thank God I didn't have to go into the office since I was on call and could work from home. The only thing I had to do this morning was to get the kids off to school.

I sat there with the phone in my hand, contemplating what to say, but decided to just wait the extra hour to get the kids off to school and then call her. At least I could speak to her un - interrupted. The entire time that I lay there, I just imagined her touching me and replaying the entire night. Why the hell am I doing that? The kids got up and got dressed after a lot of mayhem; they hated to wake up in the mornings. No matter how early they went to bed waking up was always a problem. The van driver came; I walked them out, went back in and collapsed on the couch. Just as I was about to call Zayle, a text came through:

Z- Hey morning, I thought you were going to call me☺
Me- Hey morning, Im sorry I was just about to call u ☺
Z- R u alone? Can I call u now?
Me- Yes

The phone rang and it was her.

"Hey babe. How are you? Did you sleep well?"

"Zaye, you would not believe the shit I had to go through when I got home. Darren was in here acting the fool!"

"Nai, what happened?"

"No he was just questioning me about where I was coming from and on and on?"

"But Nai, didn't you just catch him in some shit?"

"Yes I did. He has some damn nerves!" I yelled.

"Babe, don't even stress yourself out. Listen on a lighter note, how do you feel about what happened last night, honestly?"

I started to blush and giggle. Hell, I almost spat out the juice I was drinking, "Huh?"

She started to laugh. "Huh? You heard me, and be honest."

"You know what, I am not going to lie, it felt good."

"Were you comfortable, with me?"

"Zaye, I've known you for years why wouldn't I be comfortable with you?"

"Nai, it's not that. You're used to being with men, so I just wanted to know."

"You know something Zaye, you felt like a man."

We both broke out into hysterical laughter. In the midst of my conversation I hear my door open. "Zaye, let me call you back please."

"No problem, I'll be in court so call me after 4pm"

"Ok, bye."

As soon as I could shut down the cell, here comes Darren,

"So who were you speaking to huh?"

"Darren, please, why don't you leave me alone? Go to Long Island!"

"Naia, stop the bullshit I made a mistake, let me make love to you… stop this."

"Are you fucking serious Darren?"

He grabs my hand and starts trying to hug me touching my ass. Usually I could get through it. I mean many times as he was touching me or fucking me, because making love went out the door once I found out about Sophia, I would just blank out and disconnect myself and get through it. But this time I couldn't. I just went in my room and locked the door. Now not only did I not want him to make love to me, but how could I after just sleeping with Zaye. There was no way that I could do that. Not that I owed her anything, I just couldn't, and I didn't want to.

Dahlia kept calling and I just sent her to voice mail. There was no way I could explain everything to her right now, so what was the point of answering her calls. She would understand when I finally tell her everything.

All of a sudden I miss Zayle. I wish she would call me. I needed someone to talk to. Usually it was Dahlia that I would call right away but all of a sudden I wanted to speak to Zaye.

This is not good. Am I getting attached already?

Chapter 6

After the discussion Zaye and I had I decided in my mind to chalk it up to experience and left it at that. My shift at work started at 10 a.m. so I had to be up and get the kids out by 7:30 a.m. the latest, to get to work on time. At 6:30 a.m. my phone goes off and it's a text from Zaye:

Z -Good Morning

I answer her back and we start a conversation. This would become our daily routine. Unless of course things are good at home with her, then I never seem to get a text back or I get them back up to eight hours later.

Now I'm not psychic but people have patterns and her pattern was whenever things were going "good", she was "partying", or she was wining her court cases left and right, I was a distant thought. We spoke about it numerous times, but as you go along in life you will see that patterns rarely change, if they ever do at all. Oh people may change for a quick second, meaning for a couple of weeks, but they will eventually change back.

We began talking and texting every single day from sun up to sun down. The only time I wouldn't text or call was when I was with a patient. The only time that she wouldn't text or call was when she was in a trial or with a client. I would even text when Darren was at my house. Texting in the dark and in the bathroom became second nature. Although he moved, I was glad that he stuck to his agreement to baby-sit the kids for me while I covered my shifts. The only downside is that when I came in late he would already be sleeping on the couch.

Zaye and I talked about everything: dreams, fears, you name it. Talking got us through the problems that we were both experiencing in our separate homes. It was funny and co-incidental that we would be going through something at the same time. Lately we would just meet up and hang out, nothing sexual, just a lot of talking either at my house or her house, even when Suzanne was there. It ended up becoming an everyday routine. I would finish my shift, text her, and tell her I am heading home. She would text back, tell me what time her trial would end, and I guess who ever would get home first the other would meet them there.

My children were almost always at my mother's house due to my long hours and constant shift change. Thank God that she loved spending time with them. She loved to take them overnight if Darren couldn't or wouldn't keep them. That was a blessing to me, at least I was able to save that money, and put it towards paying down my school loans. Hopefully one day I will be out from under that debt.

I am at work and I am tired as hell. It is back to school season and just about every single child in the practice was scheduled for their back to school check up. Two of the doctors were out and I was the covering pediatrician. I was even more tired from all the constant arguing with Darren over the bills. Although I was a doctor I was up to my neck in school loans and credit card bills. The only three things that were up to date were my rent, my cell phone bill, and my car note. I was not about to be homeless, I needed my cell phone for work, and I sure as hell was not going to lose my Mercedes Benz.

I was in the room with a double check up giving vaccinations when I felt my pager go off. I couldn't stop to check it but then my cell phone rang and the tone for text messages ring.

Before I could pardon myself to leave the room, the overhead pager goes off "Paging Dr. Williams, line 9." I grabbed the line and answered, "Dr. Williams here." I hear on the other end, "Baby I need you, I need you now please", it's Zaye and she's crying.

"What happened? Where are you? Talk to me."
She's crying so hard that I could barely understand her.

"Where are you?" I ask again.

"I'm in the house… Please come now, I need you."

I tell her that I am on my way. I finish up my check up and immediately go into the senior doctor's office and tell him that I have a family emergency. Luckily I worked in a private practice that ran like a hospital so there was always a doctor on call. I jumped in my car and sped down the highway all the way there calling and texting her but no response. I am leaving messages, 'Please Baby, answer me, what's wrong talk to me", no answer.

It seemed like five hours later, although in actuality it was about an hour when I pulled up into her driveway. It's dark outside because it is winter and even though it was 5:30 p.m. it looked as if it was 10:30 p.m. I knocked on her door and she opens it with a bottle of champagne in one hand and a blunt in the other, and she motions for me to come in. As I walk in, she motions for me to go to the kitchen and on the table was a few letters. I look at her confused and she motioned for me to read them. There was a bank account statement with a balance of fifteen hundred dollars. It also showed a withdrawal of   thirty-five thousand. There also was an American Express bill for seven thousand dollars, a Master Card bill of two thousand dollars, and a bank letter stating that her mortgage was late.

"Oh my God babe, what happened?" I asked in shock.

"I don't know what this bitch did with my money! I found all these letters sticking behind all the shoe boxes in the closet. I just happened to find them because I was looking for my boots. I am calling her and she's not answering her phone. I am going to fuck her up!"

I'm sitting there in disbelief, "Babe what are you going to do?" I was nervous but I had to ask her, 'Do you have any other money?"

"Yes but they are in CD's," she explains.

Shit!

We sat there for an hour trying to make calls and straighten shit out, which was really pointless due to the time of evening. She kept pacing back and forth. I swore that she was going to wear out the soles of her slippers.

"What is going on Zayle? Why are you pacing?"

"Nai, you wouldn't even understand if I told you."

"Zayle try to explain it to me then. Please, it will be ok. You can make payment arrangements with all the creditors."

Her cell phone kept going off, until she threw it across the room. "Zayle, what the hell is wrong with you? You're scaring me."

"Anaiyah, I am in trouble. You wouldn't understand even if I told you."

I pull out a chair and took a seat, "Go ahead, I am listening. I am not as naive as you think I am. Did you hurt Suzanne?"

"Hell no, that bitch is not worth me spending any time behind no fucking bars!" At the same time, her house phone starts ringing. The answering machine picked up. A raspy voice came across. "Zayle don't fucking play with me! Yo meet me at the spot at 12:30, don't let me have to fucking come to your house!"

"Zayle. What the fuck is that about?" I asked.

"Listen, all you need to know is that I owe a friend money."
"Zayle, that doesn't sound like a friend!"

"Damn Anaiyah, stop fucking questioning me! Fuck!"

"You know what Zayle, FUCK YOU! I don't need this shit!" She grabs my pocket book and pulls me back. "No wait, wait... I'm in trouble ok."

"What kind of trouble?"

"I grew up with a guy on my block, Supreme. The year I entered law school, he got locked up. He had to do ten to fifteen. He gave me fifty thousand dollars to hold for him, with the agreement that when he came home he would get every single penny."

"OK, I don't understand... If you knew you were going to practice law, why would you do that?"

"I needed to supplement my school fees. Even though I got a scholarship, it was partial, and now Suzanne fucked up the money. That's how I even knew the money was missing; I went to the bank to withdraw it."

I couldn't say anything. I just sat there in disbelief.

"Naia, he's a killer, and he's pissed. I've been avoiding him and his calls for four weeks now."

I said fuck it and pulled out my check book, and wrote out checks for each bill one by one, I didn't have it but this is my best friend and I love her so much, why not? She would do it for me. She couldn't believe that I was really doing this for her. She agreed to pay me back as soon as she untied her money from the CD'S and thanked me. I stayed with her until she fell asleep on the couch and then decided to head home. I didn't wake her up; I decided to just let myself out. I made sure that her slam lock was on and double-checked that the door was locked before I headed to my car.

All the way to my house my cell kept on ringing, it was Darren as usual. I didn't even bother to answer him. On the way home, I decided to stop to get some *"McDonald's,"* wondering if I was out of my fucking mind. We were really good friends. Hell it's been six months since the night we slept together and though we've been tempted we haven't slept together since, so why in the hell did I just lend her so much money?

I got home and as usual the kids were by my mother. Sometimes this was a blessing but the house always seemed so empty without them. I called the girls and spent over an hour helping them with their homework. As soon as I finished, Zayle beeped in. It was as if she timed me.

"Hey babe, why didn't you wake me?"

"Zaye you looked so tired, I decided to let you sleep."

"Did you eat dinner yet? I am coming over."

"No I didn't eat. Come on over then."

I didn't care that she was coming over; hell I was looking forward to the company anyway. I straightened up a bit, sprayed some air freshener and jumped into the shower. By the time I came out she was knocking at my door.
"I'm coming!!" I yell running to open the door. As soon as I opened it I ran back to my room to put some clothes on.

Poor thing looked exhausted. She came in with the Chinese food and I motion for her to come into my bedroom. Usually we would just sit in the living room until we both fell asleep, but tonight I was tired too so she could come into my room. The sex issue never came up again either since the *"Marriott"*. We agreed to just be friends, which was more important to us than sex.

We ate our Chinese food and started to argue over whom would get the remote. She wanted to watch the basketball game, and I wanted to watch *"Law and Order"*. We wrestled deciding to toss a coin for it. She won.

"Zaye...please it's a new episode" I said mustering up my best whining voice.

"Won't work my dear, I won fair and square"; she said laughing at me.

I didn't even bother to stay up and try to watch the game with her. It was pointless since I didn't understand the game anyway. I cheered for whom she cheered for and booed when she booed. I was a "girly" girl, as she would always tease me.

Before I knew it I was hearing "Jay Leno" in the background. I woke up to find her on the lap top, clickety clacking away.

"Baby, what are you doing at this time on the internet?"

"Aww, It's a surprise for you." she continued, "Pass me your palm pilot. Do you still keep your work schedule in there?"

I grab my *"Blackberry"* cellular phone, enter the pass code and hand it to her wondering what in the world did she want it for. I headed in the bathroom to brush my teeth; we weren't together long enough for her to smell my morning breath at night.

"BABY! YOU HAVE A PASSPORT RIGHT?" she yelled.

I crack the bathroom door and yell back at her; "YEAH BABY, I HAVE ONE WHY?!"

She never answered me. I headed back in to the bedroom to find my bikini, laid out on the bed.

"Zaye? You plan to model this for me?" I said grinning from ear to ear knowing damn well that she would sooner walk bare foot across a fire pit than put on a bikini.

"No baby, do me a favor. Try this on for me and let me see what you look like in a bikini." I put it on and made a mental note to run and not walk to my next *"Brazilian Wax"* appointment.

"WOW! Babe you will look really nice in HAWAII!!"

"HAWAII?" I started jumping and screaming all over the room. I don't know how I didn't wake up my neighbors.

"HAWAII!!"

"Naia, you have been so loving towards me, and caring and patient. Our birthdays are a week apart, why not celebrate them together?"

"But, Zaye, I thought we were going to get together and have an all white party, valet parking and everything?"

"NAH! FUCK A PARTY! Let's go away... I've always wanted to go." I didn't know what to say, no one has ever done anything this nice for me ever.

"Zaye, when do we leave?"

"Start packing your bags, I am going home to pack I will see you in the morning at the airport."

"WHAT?", I looked at her in amazement.

"I took the liberty of checking your phone, so I know you're off for the next two weeks, and the kids are going with your mother to Maryland for the two weeks starting tomorrow."

I jumped up and hugged her. I couldn't believe this was really happening. It was crazy. Every man I have ever been with has always planned all kinds of trips for me and they never came through. I cannot believe it took a WOMAN to do this for me.

Not to mention the time Darren told me we were going away. I planned and coordinated babysitters for him to tell me at the last minute that we weren't going because he had an emergency at work. Months later I found out that the emergency was that he didn't even book a ticket.

The time before that I was dating a guy in med school and he swore he was in love with me. He asked me to take a vacation with him but we decided to go half and half. The deal was I would purchase the tickets and he would pay for the hotel rooms.

Well right up until the night before, we were all set and ready to go. Until I received the call, almost exact to Darren's that he had an emergency at work. My money was lost and my pride injured.

She left and I headed to start packing my bags. They say the third time is the charm. Or is it?

HAWAII HERE I COME!

Chapter 7

We agreed to meet at my house and share a cab to *"JFK"* airport. It was much easier than either one of us driving there and then leaving our jeeps in the extended parking area. We spoke early in the morning around 3:00 am and agreed to meet at 5:00 am. Our flight was scheduled to leave at 11am, and with all the new added security measures that were now implemented at the airport, it was suggested we arrive a couple of hours early.

I woke up, checked my bags to make sure that I had everything that I planned to take with me and made sure that all my new Victoria Secret negligees were packed and ready to go. New underwear …check, new bras…check, new night gown check. I threw in a few g-strings just in case we had somewhere to go if we found time to leave the room, which I seriously doubted….but who knew, stranger things have happened.

I woke up and called her, no answer, but that didn't alarm me. As I have said before she has been known to not hear her phone when it goes off. While I was in the shower, I heard my phone go off and when I reached for it there was a text: Hey baby..can't wait to see u, im in the shower now..ill c u at the airport..don't wait for me..ill meet u there.. Hawaii..here we cum..luv u ☺

I smiled with excitement, jumped out the shower and dried myself off. I brought along a sexy Juicy Couture jump suit and Hogan sneakers since she always commented on how she loved to see me in sportswear.

I sprayed on her favorite perfume, called the kids to tell them that I was passing by my mom's house to kiss them and see them before they went to school and before
I headed for the airport, and called a cab. On my way to see the kids, I text her: Baby ..on my way to c the kids..will text u when I reach JFK…luv u !!

 I got to my mom's house in less than five minutes kissed the kids, told them I loved them and headed to John F. Kennedy airport. I got there within twenty minutes, as we pulled up into the circular drop off area I text her again: baby..im here..meet me at Starbucks..luv u.

I checked in my bags and went and to get us a seat in Starbucks. An hour passed and I got no text or phone call. Again I'm not alarmed; I mean why should I be? She paid almost two thousand dollars for our tickets and a grand for our rooms. Why would she waste it? Plus she wouldn't do this to me would she? Stand me up for a trip …nah…no way. It's thirty minutes until boarding time. I start to panic and call Dahlia. "Dee. It's 30mins till boarding time and she's not here…do you think something happened?"

"No call her, I'm sure she's on her way….Naia don't panic she'll show up," Dahlia promised.

"But Dee, it's thirty minutes till boarding. She should have been here already."

"Naia, u know Zayle is always late! Just be patient. She'll show up. Stay calm."

"Ok, if u say so."

Thirty minutes passed and now they're calling to board our flight.

I'm calling her and calling her and I am not getting any answer. This can't be happening! No way, something must have happened to her.

There's no way she would do this! Our birthdays are coming up... I called and texted to no avail. "Last call for *"American Airline"*, flight 308 to Honolulu Hawaii."

"Oh my God this can't be happening!"

I call her frantically; "Baby, please where are you? The flight is boarding and they just called for the last call. Please! Where are u?" Still; no answer. This IS really happening I drop my pocket book and slump to the floor to begin to cry. Ok let me get myself together, maybe something is wrong with her? Maybe she got in an accident on her way here? OH my God I would never forgive myself if something happened to her on her way here. An airport employee came over to me, "Ma'am? Are you ok? Can I help you? Do you need me to call someone for you?"

Through my tears I replied, "No...I'm ok thank you."

Now I'm crying uncontrollably. I am too embarrassed to call Dahlia to come and get me from the airport. I mean come on what am I going to say. But I have an even bigger problem my entire luggage was already checked in and on its way to Hawaii. I should've boarded the plane, and said, "Fuck her", and just go. I mean how the hell could she do this to me? But I decide first let me make sure that she is ok. She always said I had a bad habit of jumping to conclusions before I knew if everything was ok, when she would pull a disappearing acts on me before... but I can't lie this would be the last straw.

I picked myself up, tried to dry my tears, and walked out to hail a cab. Where was I going to go? Everyone knew I was supposed to be going to Hawaii. She only planned it the evening before, but I was so excited I told everyone.

I told the cabbie my address. Let me go home first, maybe something happened.

I'm just hoping that it was nothing bad and that she was physically ok, because then I could kill her. All the way home, I called her ...no answer. Just her voice mail... "Hi, this is Zayle I am unable to take your call right now, if this is a client please call me on 718-555-1212, and I will return your call in order of priority."

"Ok what the fuck, I am a priority right now! Answer your fucking phone Zayle I'm not playing with you! Please call or text me right fucking now, how could you do this to me?" I hung up furious. Still all the way home no answer no text.

I get home, fling open my door and head straight to my bed. I threw myself across it and started to cry so hard that I thought my heart was going to literally come out of my chest. All I kept thinking was why would she do this to me? How could she do this to me? Me of all people!? I thought she said she loved me and would do anything in the world for me... She promised to never hurt me. So what is going on?

As I'm lying there my cell phone starts ringing off the hook. It's only Dahlia, wishing me a safe flight and telling me to call her once I land. Yeah right. I tuned off my phone, but quickly turned it back on. What if she's hurt? What if she needs me? But at the same time I'm thinking, "Fuck her! She left me at the airport."

I call her after now six hours later and leave her another message letting her know that I cannot believe that she did this and that it was over. "I can't keep going through this with you anymore! You are mean and you obviously don't care anything about my feelings or me! You will miss me when I'm gone Zayle!" I explained. Still; no answer or text.

I'm beginning to worry. I call her mom, her sister and even her brother, but hung up after they answered. I figured if she were hurt at least one of them would call me since they thought we were in a relationship and as crazy as it was, we never confirmed or denied it. We never had to. I didn't want to alarm them with any questions because they also knew we were supposed to be in Hawaii. I decided, I needed to take a warm bath, lie down and relax myself.

I had a splitting migraine and my eyes were beginning to swell from all the crying that I had done in the past six hours or so. I didn't even know what time it was. It seemed like an entire day had passed.

I turned on some music, which unfortunately had to be CDs that she made for me because that was all I had. I didn't want to hear any hip-hop or commercials right now so I decided to just let the CDs play. I guess Dahlia called the hotel for me, and they told her I didn't check in. My answering machine and cell phone machine was filled with messages. She was worried. I don't want to answer because I feel like a fucking fool. How could she do this to me? My God! She actually made me go to airport. She paid all this money for us to go away, and then stood me up?

Dahlia's voice came over the answering machine, "NAIA, honey please if you are there I am worried about you. Please answer me."

I pick up. "Hey, just come over please…"

She started to talk anyway but I interrupted her and told her "Please I don't feel like talking, just come over," and hung up the phone.

I lay across my couch wondering when and how did I get so caught up in Zayle that she was now playing me for a fool and embarrassing me.

This is it; I am done with her. No more. Thank God Dahlia had a spare key, because I really didn't feel like getting up to open no damn door. She walked in and came over to me, except she had a mixed look of anger and disgust on her face. I really didn't know what to think. She told me to have a seat. The first thing that came to my mind was oh shit, something is wrong with Zayle.

"Dee what is it? Tell me! Is something wrong with Zayle? TELL ME!"

"Nai sit down. No nothing is wrong with her, but sit down."

"DAHLIA TALK TO ME NOW!" I screamed. I am terrified at this point. Did I jump to conclusions once again? Is my baby hurt?

"Anaiyah, I drove past Zayle's house and they are having a party."

"A WHAT!?"

"A party!" she confirmed.

"Dahlia go and find something in my closet and get dressed, we are going over there!"

She tried to convince me not to go over there, but she knew there was no talking to me at this point. She told me that all of the guests that she saw walking into her backyard had on white. I went into my closet and threw her a white skirt and a sexy white top. I'm so angry and so filled with rage.

I stand under the shower for twenty minutes. To let the water run threw my hair, trying to calm myself down. This bitch is crazy. Is she really having an all white party?

The same party that I begged her to let us have together and she told me that she would rather us take a trip to Hawaii. She said she always wanted to go and that I am the person she wanted to go with. We got dressed and headed out. All the way there, Dahlia is trying to convince me to turn back but I am not even going to answer her.

I held my head straight. As soon as we pulled into her driveway, I hopped out of the car, threw the keys to the valet person and marched my ass across the front lawn, making my way to the backyard filled with people. She was too busy looking into Suzanne's eyes to even see me. I walked in as Suzanne was toasting her. "To my lovely wife, who means the world to me: Happy Birthday, I love you."

She leaned in, whispered "I love you too," the crowd cheered and clapped. I clapped too. Shit what the hell else am I to do?

As I approached her, her best friend Tee, otherwise known as Tione, saw me and tried to run intervention. I guess she watched too many football games, and really did not know me well enough to know that there is no way she was stopping me. Tione had the nerve to grab my hand. "Tee, if you don't get off of my hand, I will cut you, I swear I will!"
I walked right up to her back, and tapped her on her shoulder. I hugged Suzanne and told her "Hi".

 Zayle put the bottle of *"Moet"* straight to her head; I am surprised that she didn't choke.

"HAPPY BIRTHDAY!" I yelled at her. She couldn't even respond, she just kept chugging away at the bottle. "I love your party, great job!"

Suzanne excused herself to go get some more liquor. That's when I slapped her dead across her face. I couldn't help it.

"How, fucking dare you Zayle? You're a fucking bitch!" I threw my glass at her and walked away.

Here goes this bitch Tione running behind me. "Tee, get away from me! Go and tell Zayle I said have a happy fucking life!"

At this point I just wanted to get home. Dahlia, knew me well enough to know that she had better be in front of me on the driver's side of the car or directly behind me, by the time I got there, or she would be left right there in the party. I stayed silent the entire drive home. I drove straight to Dahlia's house and dropped her home. I didn't hear anything she said to me, I just saw her lips moving. I caught myself speeding, driving at nearly ninety miles an hour. "Shit! I better slow down, this bitch is not worth me getting a speeding ticket or points on my license, much less killing myself... Hell no!"

I get in my house and strip. I grab my favorite silk kimono, and look at myself in the mirror. I am a beautiful woman, smart, sexy, and I have a fantastic career. Who in their right mind wouldn't want me? Everything down to my toes are pretty. Perfectly aligned, no corns, no dark toenails. So what is the problem? Why don't I have someone who loves me, and can put me first in their life? Thank God for music. It is so true the old saying that music soothes the beast. Every single time that I am angry or frustrated, I just play some music and it magically soothes me.

Maybe I should just be a bitch? Maybe I should just go find some man to fuck and get over her? Maybe I should find some woman to just fuck and get over her? Who knows, maybe it's better to just fuck myself.

I had to laugh at myself. I was actually starting to feel a little better, until I heard my answering machine pick up.

"Anaiyah, this is your mother, please call me once you get to your hotel room. I need to speak with you. I hope it is not true what I am hearing that you went to Hawaii with that dyke friend of yours."

Oh good, now I have to deal with her shit. When will she stop caring about what everyone else thinks, and just care about me? Does it really matter who makes me happy?

Then there is a knock at my door.

"WHO THE HELL IS IT?"

"Naia, it's me Tee."

"Tee, if Zayle is with you tell her to go home to her bitch!"

"Nah, Nai, I'm alone."

I opened the door. She stepped right in as if I had invited her.

"Tee, what do you want? I really don't want to hear anything Zayle has to say."

"No, Naia, I'm here to make sure your ok. Come sit down and talk to me."

She takes a seat on my couch, again as if I invited her. Why would I want to speak to her? She was at the party, and I'm sure she was laughing behind my back.

"Naia, listen, what Zayle did to you was fucked up. You need someone like me in your life. I'll take care of you. I told her what she was doing was fucked up."

"Excuse me Tionne, but who do you think you're talking to? You're a fucked up person to come in here, drop dime on your friend, and then turn around and try to kick it to me. GET OUT!"

My cell and house phone would not stop ringing. It's Zayle now and she is ringing my phone off the hook. What could she possibly have to say to me?

"Tionne, please leave my house immediately!" Before I could even finish my sentence, my front door busts open.

"OH OK! NOW I SEE WHY YOU'RE NOT ANSWERING MY CALLS... YOU'RE FUCKED UP NAIA!"

Zayle just bursts in my door. I gave her an emergency key, after Darren moved out.

"Zayle, are you kidding me? Please tell your friend to leave my house, and ask her to tell you everything she told me on your way out."

"NAH, you guys have a good night. It's obvious I interrupted a romantic rendezvous." Tionne then looks at Zayle and lies straight through her teeth.

"Son, she called me over crying. I came to check on her."

"Excuse me T, what did you just say? You're a liar!"

Zayle looked at me and shook her head. As if she was disgusted with me.

"Zayle I know there is no way that your believing this chick, you know me."

Tionne starts to yell at the top of her voice. "Yo son, she's lying! She called me saying how upset she was and invited me over."

I threw the bottle of wine that I was drinking straight at her head, and then took both my house phone and cell phone and slapped Zayle in her chest with it.

"Look at the call logs! Do you see that I made any calls to this woman? Do you?"

She looked me straight in the eyes, and asked me, "Nai, did you call T over here?"

"No!"

All of a sudden, an evil face came over her and she grabbed Tionne by her shirt collar. They started to scuffle and knock my lamps over. There was no way I was getting involved. Fuck them both. The next thing I knew, Zayle threw Tionne out of my house, punched her square in the nose, and then slammed the door in her face.

I sat on the couch. There were no words for me to say. She just sat there looking at me as if she were hurt. There was no way that I was giving here any sympathy. I mean come on she just left my ass at the airport. She didn't even have the decency to call and tell me a lie.

If there was any justification to being told a lie, this was one of the times I would probably have appreciated being lied to. At least my heart would have appreciated it.

I pushed her off of me as soon as she leaned in to kiss me. Is she crazy? She never said a word. She just started to undress me and of course I let her. I am such a fool! In my head I'm saying, "Stop! Get off of me! You don't deserve me!

You're no good for me!" but the words wouldn't cross my lips. Am I so desperate to feel loved? To feel like I won?

Suzanne is at the white party waiting for her, but where is she? She's right here with me. What I really needed to remember was the saying that I told all of my friends, "Sometimes when you think you lose, you really win."

She kept on until I was fully undressed. She kissed every single part of my body. I had never seen her this way before.

It wasn't the liquor because we've made love before, while she was drunk but this was different. In my head I interpreted that she was apologizing. The only words that crossed her lips were after I came in her mouth. "I love you, please forgive me. Please don't leave me, I need you!" she begged.

I replied, "How many times will I have to forgive you?"

She silenced me with a kiss.

Chapter 8

She walked out just like that. It was as if nothing happened a few hours before. I still had to deal with the fact that my entire luggage was in Hawaii and I was still here in Brooklyn, NY. I also had to deal with the fact that I looked and felt like a fool, idiot and an asshole. Everything that "T" said the night before was true, but she had her own agenda for telling me. It's not as if she was telling me because she cared. The phone started ringing at 6 am sharp. Everyone from Dahlia to Zayle's mom was calling me to find out if I was ok? Hell no I'm not ok! Zayle has my life in a freaking uproar right now. I look like a fool.

How am I to explain to everyone that they were right all along? She was only playing with my feelings and emotions and just using me as a pacifier for when shit wasn't right at home. But as usual I fall for the apology, the tears and the showy display of affection.

I hear my front door open and its Darren. God damn it I can't get a fucking moment to myself. I told him that I was going away with Dahlia, so now I have to explain why the hell I'm still home. Shit I have to think fast.
He walks in "What the hell are you doing here? Why are you not in Hawaii?" with a smirk on his face.

I blurted out the first thing I could think… "Dahlia had a patient that committed suicide, a minor, and they paged her while we were at the airport."

I had to move fast. I grabbed my cell phone and ran into the bathroom blurting out that I had to shit, just to be able to text Dahlia and tell her not to come over here saying anything else to the contrary and to act sad if she did come over here. She didn't respond so I knew she was sleeping.

"How did you get in?" I asked him.

"You forgot you left me the key to come in and get any extra stuff that your mother might have needed me to send? But since your home, I don't need you to take them anymore, do I?"

"Darren, Dee is going through some stuff right now. She needs a friend and she is feeling guilty about this girl. Please just keep them so I can be there for her. Is that hard?" God he always acts like I don't need a moment for myself.

He starts to walk over to me and I know its sex he wants. He always wants sex but I can't. My mind is far away from this moment in time. It's still on what happened last night, how I got played at the party, how she fought "Tione" and threw her out of my house, how she made love to me and just got up and left as if nothing happened.

Darren walks over and tries to kiss me. I back him off and tell him that I am not in the mood. He catches an attitude and screams "You're never in the mood."

I really don't feel like arguing with him. It is too early in the morning, I have a hangover and I want to sleep. Thank God I don't have to work today. He continues to go on and on about how I don't love him and don't want to give him any sex and how I am treating him badly. Now I'm angry and get on the defensive.

"Darren, do you not see all the bills I have piled up because of my school loans? Not to mention I'm a little upset because I'm supposed to be in Hawaii, and all you're thinking about is sex, and your feelings."

Conveniently his phone rings and he hits ignore. I look at him and smirk. He looks back at me and laughs.

"Who is on the phone Darren?

"Why do you care? You're not fucking me?" With that I ask him to leave my house, immediately. He turns, walks out and slams my door.

I decided to call the airlines to ask them about the process of getting my luggage returned to New York. I had a few new pieces of couture in there that I really didn't want to risk losing. While on the phone with them, I started to think, I had a lot of time to think since I was transferred between recordings and live operators for about 60 minutes.

I decided that I had to figure out what exactly I wanted in my life. Did I want to continue to play this back and forth game with Zayle, being her band-aid whenever she felt as if she needed me? She didn't want to be in an exclusive relationship with me. I think that was because she knew that the shit that she was able to get away with Suzanne, she would never be able to get away with me.

Not because I am super woman, but just simply being sober, would be enough to change Zayle's game. I even discussed with her that being with me, would change her life dramatically because I have kids. It would have to be more of a calmer life, which is why I chose to work in a private practice and not a hospital, to be able to structure my hours around my children.

She always said yes, this is what she wants, to settle down and be a family. She explained she was tired of partying Friday to Sunday. I mean the girl lives to party. She and Suzanne are at every party and club you can think of every weekend. She has even been so drunk after partying on a Sunday that she missed jury selection for one of her clients. Of course naturally I gave her a doctor's note and saved her ass from being fired.

Why do I care so much about her? She's only really nice to me 50% of the time. Either she has a new girlfriend, or when she and Suzanne are at war that is when I get treated best.
She'll surprise me at work for lunch, I'll get a thousand text messages or she will surprise me and pick me up to take me to work or pick me up from work. I even get phone calls with five-hour conversations but as soon as she and Suzanne are good and at peace, I get none of the above. I can barely hear from her, no phone calls or anything…I could call until I'm blue in the face. She will respond to my texts up to 8 hrs later. So why do I go through this?

Then Darren, he's just as bad. His phone goes off all hours of the night when he stays over at my house. When I check his voicemail, I even hear his "baby mama" arguing because he was suppose to drop the car off for her at a certain time and he didn't. Now my thing is this, why is she able to curse you out about "your" car? To make it worse, thank God I have my own car; because this man argues every single solitary time I ask him for a ride anywhere. It could be to do something for his own children, it doesn't matter, he's bugging me to hurry up and get into the car, rushing me wherever we are, hurrying me, complaining about gas the entire way and that he is not a taxi service. This is every single time I get into his car. But, you are willing to lend your baby mother your car?

Why am I settling and playing games with both of these assholes? Neither one of them love me. They're just comfortable with me and don't want anyone else to have me. That has to be it. In the middle of my mental debate with myself, I forgot I was still holding on with the airport, when Dahlia beeps in.

"Hey, get up get dressed and come over here. I have some friends I would like you to meet."

"Ok, just let me get off of the pone with the airline, and.."
Before I could finish my sentence, she interjects "Naia, you will be on the phone with those people until next year. Just give it up and wait for them to just call you, and tell you that they have your luggage, you will save a few gray hairs."

"Gray hair? Speak for yourself bitch!" I told her I would pass by.

When I arrived at her house they were heading out to get something to eat. As I walked in the door, she quickly did the introductions. The only introduction that caught my eye was Warren. Warren and I happened to be trying to pass through the door at the same time and we got stuck. We both started to laugh and I looked into his eyes and they were this amazing blue, almost turquoise hue. Now what made them so beautiful was the fact that his complexion was dark, almost ebony. "Wow!" After I stared at him for about ten seconds I glanced away.

"You guys plan on staying stuck like that or do you intend on moving out of the way so we can leave!?" Dahlia asked us. We both laughed. I pushed my way passed the awkward position and continued to walk into the house towards the bedroom. They both walked in there and asked if I was going to join them for dinner.

They had to be crazy, I had on a pair of wrinkled scrubs and a pair of old ass Jordan's, where was I going? Plus with the night that I had before I really didn't feel like having fun. They insisted and of course with my hungry belly, I gave in.

I stopped at my car first and grabbed my *"Gucci"* jeans jacket, at least let me try to impress him a little bit. Let me admit, I'm a *"Gucci"* addict. Impressed he was indeed. I pulled my hair up just to make it a little neater, and tried my best to straighten out my scrubs. On our way to his car, he made it known that I would ride shotgun with him. Ok, no arguments here. I hopped into the front seat with him. As soon as we pull out of her garage, we hear a screech, breaks are being hit and we slam into the side of another car that was pulling out of a parking space on the street.

His hand flew across my chest as if to hold me back, as crazy as this sounds now, I was impressed. He didn't know me from a hole in the wall but was concerned of my safety. We were ok just a little shaken up, but more importantly no one was hurt. We all exited the cars including the passengers from the other car. The two drivers stood there and argued over whose fault it was and after they couldn't come to an agreement; they decided to call the police.

I saw Warren walk to the back of the car and signaled me over with just a look, no words, and no motions, just a look. As I walked over to him, he took me by my hands and asked if I was ok. While holding my hands, he slipped something in to my hand. I pushed my hands in to my pocket, explained to everyone that I had to pee, and walked off to the house, never looking back. As I entered the house, I pushed my hand in my pocket and pulled out what he gave me. It was a plastic bag full of weed.

I wasn't shocked since I knew Dahlia smoked also. I was annoyed that she allowed me to get into the car risking my medical license and my job, knowing that there was weed in the car. It was all done and over with already so I rested it on the dresser in her guest room and went to lie down in her room.

As I lay down in her room I heard everyone come back into the house. Warren and his friends were pretty pissed off as anyone could imagine but at the same time he was so cool about it. His smoothness and demeanor impressed me. He even spoke calmly, not raising his voice once, except for when he and the other driver were debating over whose fault it was. He came over and sat beside me, "Are you ok?"

At the same time my pager went off. It was the answering service, even though I was not on call that night, they were paging me to tell me that one of my patients, had a fever of 103.3 and that the parents suspected strep throat. I called the parents back and told them to meet the on call doctor at the office, that they would get a call from the doctor, telling them what time the appointment would be for. The on call doctor didn't have to actually stay at the office and wait for a patient to call in on weekends. They would call the answering service that would in turn notify us of the patient's symptoms. Then the doctor on call would call the patient back and tell them what time to meet us in the office.

"Everything ok?" Dahlia asked since she knew that 9 out of ten times when my pager went off it meant I had to leave.

"Is that a patient? Do you have to leave?"

"I'll take you, where do you have to go, Manhattan?" Warren asked with what sounded like he actually hoped I had to leave.

"No, but if you plan to take me out, that would be fine too."

"That's not a problem lets go".

"Yes, but we're taking my car." We all laughed and I threw him the keys, while asking him if he even knew Manhattan.

"I use to live in Manhattan, Missy!" he said while winking at me. I kissed Dahlia and told her that we would be back. We jumped into my jeep and drove off. He commented on the fact that he liked my *"Benz"* and the next thing I knew he was asking me who I was fighting in my sleep. I fell asleep while he was driving to the city which was unusual for me because not even when Dahlia drove did I ever go to sleep, much less a stranger.

He pulled over into a parking space gave me an envelope; and told me to go into the store and buy a change of clothes, the plans have changed. "Nothing dressy, just some jeans a top and some shoes."

I was in shock. No one ever does stuff like this for me. I am the one who does stuff like this for people, never the other way around. My first instinct was to hand him back his money and use my own charge card. Then I remembered I hadn't paid the bill this month. I sent a large check to my student loan so that they wouldn't garnish my wages. I am now living on a 'budget'.

He leaned across me and opened the passenger door, and told me to go ahead. "I'll circle back in a half hour but if I'm not out there when you come back call me on your cell phone."

That's when I remembered we never exchanged phone numbers. "I don't have your number," I explained.

"Dial 561-555-8247."

I dialed it and when the number dialed on my phone it registered as Naia's new boyfriend.

Chapter 9

started to laugh and blush, then he turned his phone around to show me his phone. Displayed on the cell phone screen "Warren's new girlfriend". I found myself giggling like a teenager but I had to play it cool. I turned around and walked off into the store. He must have wanted me to dress casually because he sent me into Armani Exchange. As soon as I walked in, I called Dahlia.

"Girl, do you know he just handed me an envelope and sent me into Armani Exchange, to shop!"

"How much did he give you?"

"I don't know, I didn't count it."

"Girl you better count it!", she yelled into the cell phone.

I opened the envelope it was filled with fifty dollar bills, thirty to be exact.

"Oh my God, its fifteen hundred dollars in the envelope!"

"Girl, you better get to shopping!"

"I know, I know, but sidebar... Do you know that Zayle hasn't even called me?"

"Girl fuck Zayle, she dissed you! You better start shopping."

I hung up the phone and headed over to the jeans section. I figured I would wear jeans and a button down shirt since he was casually dressed also.

I still stopped to check and see if Zayle had texted or called, but still nothing. I felt disappointed but continued to shop. While shopping Darren called me but I hit ignore. He starts to text me.

Darren: Y r u ignoring my calls? U need 2 come home and get the girls. I dropped them at ur moms house. I have things to do.

I text back: What would u do if I was in Hawaii, ur an asshole. I am not picking up the kids from moms house, u go back and get them, pretend I am in Hawaii still.

Then I called Zayle. Straight to voicemail as usual but this time I didn't even bother to leave her a message. I just hung up and proceeded to shop. All the while I am aggravated. How could she treat me like this? Why is Darren such an ass? I decided to just hurry up and get out of the store as to not make a bad impression on Warren our first time out, if this would be considered our first date. I quickly found an outfit and paid for it.

Went into the dressing room and changed. I threw my scrubs in the shopping bag and hurried out of the store. As I walked out of the store, I didn't see my jeep pulling up, so I got ready to call him when I heard the horn blow.

"Hey did I take long?" I asked.

"Not at all."

I jumped in and strapped my seat belt on, and handed him back the envelope, he handed it back to me.

"That's yours, what are you doing?"

"Are you sure?", I asked.

He rolled his eyes while laughing and pulled out of the parking space. I turned sideways and asked him if he liked my choice. "Very nice!" he reassured and smiled. I chose a black v-neck button down shirt with poufy sleeves and a pair of dark blue bootleg cut jeans. I reached in the back of the car for my belt. With the hectic life I lived I always had something in the back of my car: a change of clothes, extra shoes, make up, hair products. It was a big joke with all of my friends, that if I ever got stuck somewhere, I could literally live out of my car. He noticed that I still had on my Jordan's, "What happened? You didn't see any shoes that you liked?"

"No they don't sell shoes in the *"Armani Exchange"* and I didn't want to make you wait." I couldn't tell him that I was actually preoccupied with texting a woman that I cared for more than she cared for me, and arguing with a selfish baby father. Not cool.

He pulled over after driving a few blocks looked down at my feet and told me that he would be right back. I looked to see where he was going and it looked like he ran into the corner bodega, until I realized that he went into a shoe store. "OH MY GOD, this man is not going to buy me shoes."

After ten minutes of waiting in complete and utter disbelief that this man just went to buy me shoes, he came over to the passenger side of the car and handed me the bag. I pulled out a beautiful pair of black high-heeled sandals that were simply gorgeous. The price tag said five hundred and ninety-five dollars.

This guy has style. I gave him a half hug out of the car window and then he walked around and hopped back into the car.

"Like steak?" he asked. It was hot as hell since it was August, so we closed the windows and blasted the air conditioner. We headed to the "*Gallagher's Steakhouse*." The steak I ordered was one of the juiciest that I had ever tasted. Every five minutes Dahlia would text me, just to be nosey. He noticed that my cell phone kept vibrating, "Someone is missing you huh?"

"No, no one misses me." I said while laughing, but knowing that it was true.

"Well tell them you are out with your new man," he said with a very straight face. Is this where I explain to him that I am sleeping with my best friend, who I happened to fall in love with, and oh yeah by the way it's a girl and oh yeah she lives with her woman? By the way, I have a baby father, who is just around and acts as if we are still together even though he is seeing someone else who is pregnant by him.

We continue our dinner and of course the age-old question comes up. "Are you dating anyone right now?" I didn't want to lie, but I didn't want to answer, so I flipped the question back to him. "Well are YOU dating someone right now?"

He winked at me and told me not to avoid his question, but that he liked my style, and we both started to laugh. Then I figured fuck it, why do I have to lie, I don't owe him any explanation and he doesn't owe me any. I still didn't answer, instead I said, "You first... Are you dating anyone right now?"

He replied, "Well, I was seeing someone for a while, we broke up but..."

I stopped him right there in his tracks, "Anything after 'but', is bullshit, so to just leave it alone."
"Well my situation is difficult to explain."

"What is difficult? Difficult as in you're married to a murderer?" We both cracked up laughing.

"NO!"

We both laughed so hard we didn't hear the waiter walk up and ask us if we wanted to order our desserts. I grabbed the menu hoping I was off of the hook. We both ordered our desserts. He then turned to me and told me to not even think that I was off of the hook.

"OK. OK , you may not like this though." I warned.

"Why not? Now you're making me scared." He raised one eyebrow and brought those beautiful eyes closer up to mine.

"Ok, right now I am dealing with a woman, and my daughters' father is sometimes around."

"Cool..."

"Cool? What do you mean cool?"

"So, you're bi-sexual?", he said very calmly.

"No...not really, I mean it is hard to explain", I started to get frustrated and stutter, because no one has ever put the question to me so straight forward and to the point before. Ever!

I mean I never even asked myself, that question before. I don't even think that I have an answer because I don't know myself!

I was so happy when the waiter brought the desert to the table, that I grabbed his hands as I took the plate out of his hands, startling him.

At least now, I can avoid giving an answer.

Which really was, I'm neither I'm just me.

Chapter 10

After the party Zayle promised me that we would spend more time together, and she kept her word. Everything seemed to be going fine again, I fell right back in to the trap. All was well. Even though I helped her to catch up on her mortgage, she insisted on moving anyway. She said she wanted to be closer to the kids and me and that Suzanne was finally moving out so she really didn't need a house, unless the girls and I were going to live with her. She searched for months on end. Taking me with her, to view condos and asking for my opinion, even telling me that she would put me on her lease or mortgage whichever one she finally decided to go with.

It seems as though the day had come so fast, even though I knew about it, I guess I figured that it wouldn't bother me so much since she was just moving about fifteen minutes from me. We would be able to spend time together more frequently and I would be more at ease. Except, I'm starting to feel jealous… Yes, I'm jealous of the fact that yes she is moving and it's not with me. How would I explain to my mother and everyone else that I was living with a woman, even though it really should not matter. I'm just too deep into this lie!

She tried to make me feel better. I know she even chose the condominium because of the close proximity to my home so that made me happy. Until, she called me and told me to come over. She said that she wanted me to see the place, I guess so that I wouldn't feel left out.

I went, but let me bring you up to speed. As usual we had a brutal argument the night before. She told me she wanted to see me and for us to go to the club together.

At the same time Dahlia came by and wanted to go out also, so she told me to get dressed and go with Dee and the girls. She would meet me there.

I got dressed to go, nothing fancy just some jeans and a *"Polo Ralph Lauren"* shirt and sneakers. Now I was tired but my baby wanted to see me and that is all that mattered to me. Earlier that day we were talking about going to the hotel to spend some quality time together since it had been weeks since we were able to actually get away together. With her court cases and my recent schedule change we hadn't made love or chilled out for the longest time. So we made arrangements to meet up and go to the hotel together except that when I woke up, both of my children were sick. The younger one woke up with a splitting headache saying that she felt dizzy, and my big baby woke up with stomach pains that she had been feeling for a couple of weeks. Now what am I to do?

I have to go to work since I am the doctor on call this weekend and I'm hoping to impress them so that maybe one day I will be considered for partner... I call Darren even though I know that is a waste of time but still I believe in the benefit of doubt so I call anyway. "Listen your daughters are sick, can you come by the house and pick them up and take them to work with you? Being that you've been at your job longer than me, you have days that you can take..." What does he do? Suck his teeth and say Naia I can't come by there. I just said good-bye.

When it comes to my kids there are only two people I can depend on besides my mother and that is Zayle and Dahlia.

I had to ask Dahlia to watch both my kids, which she did for me. She then drove them with my mother to meet me in Manhattan so that I could take them to their doctor's appointment.

I didn't want to bring them to my practice, not for any specific reason other than I am a private person. I left and met them for their office visit and spent two hours with them there.

I got back to the job and it dawned on me that Darren hadn't even called to see how his own children were doing. I mean my God? If I call you and tell you that they are sick, wouldn't you at least pick up the phone and call me to see how they are feeling and what happened? Asshole.....

Unlike Zayle who immediately after I texted her and tell her the kids are sick, she calls me. Before I could finish the last text message and hit send she's calling me.

"Baby what's wrong with the kids? Call the doctor and take them there. Do you need me to drive you, or take them for you?"

After reassuring her, "Baby it's ok, I'll get it done don't worry about it." She makes sure that I promise to call her and let her know exactly what the doctor said about everything. It turned out that my oldest daughter had a virus, and nothing can be done for her but give her "*Tylenol*" and wait it out. Yael my baby needed to have a blood test. Nothing major, but just to see if she was lactose intolerant and if that is why she would get stomach pains every time she drank or ate certain things.

When I called her to tell her the results she immediately cancelled our plans. I was dying to see her and was so stressed out that all I really wanted to do was make love and feel loved.

I just needed to get away from it all for a few hours, but she insisted on canceling our plans until the kids were feeling better, which also made me feel good because I know that even though she wanted to see me, she loved my kids more than she loved me and missed me. My kids came first to her also.

Later that night after my kids felt a little better, she told me to go with Dahlia and that she would leave Suzanne home and come meet me at the club. I was feeling exhausted and even though I didn't want to go I went anyway. After standing in the club and leaning on a wall like a wall flower for a few hours I accepted the fact that she was not coming.

We texted up until the very moment that I left the house. Just so that she would know that I was definitely going, but still no answer. It was too late to change my mind now. She made sure to text me and tell me that I better not have no one up in my face and to behave myself. In the middle of the party I text her and tell her "Thank you for standing me up once again."

She replies, "I didn't know you I really wanted me to come?" This pisses me off! "Hello!" I texted, " I only went because you asked me to go! What the hell are you talking about?'

"Baby I'm getting in a cab now, I'm on my way" she replies.

"Zayle why are you coming now, the party is over I am heading home."

After texting back and forth for about twenty minutes I arrive at my house tired as hell and dying to sleep. I throw myself across my bed and fall asleep.

Only to hear my phone ring in what seemed to be fifteen minutes later. It was actually hours later and my mother telling me that she could not take Saniyah to her piano lesson and that I would have to take her.

I really had no problem with that she's my child. It was just that if I knew I would have to get up early I would've gone to bed earlier. Now I am cranky and miserable.

Zayle texts me: Please don't be mad that I didn't show up. I miss you.

I text back: Just so u know, not only am I fucking pissed but I am extremely cranky and miserable right now.

She calls me, "Hey my pretty baby, what's the matter?"

The way I answered her she knew I was pissed at her. At the same time I was happy to hear from her because I was so fucking tired I felt delirious.

"Don't ask me no fucking questions, what do you want? I want to sleep! Are you sucking my pussy today or what? It's been weeks and I am sexually frustrated!" I could hear her chuckle really low…and that made me laugh but at the same time I was dead serious. Shit, time was up!

"Uh oh…Somebody needs there pussy sucked."

"Zayle don't piss me the fuck off, are you going to suck my pussy or what?"

"Yes my love, meet me at the new apartment after you drop Saniaya off ok?"

"Baby I am not gonna stay on the phone with you because I am so fucking cranky right now. I'm not responsible for what comes out my mouth and I don't want to argue with you."

"Ok baby, call me when you're on your way, I love you." She said as she laughed at me.

I call Darren to see if he can give us a ride home because my car was in the shop getting serviced and the rain started to pour down accompanied by thunder and lighting. I called a cab and waited for about forty minutes and still nothing was in the area.

"Hey Darren, can you come and give us a ride home?"

"Listen Naia I have things to do. Why don't you just call a cab?"

"Darren, don't you think I've done that? Unfortunately there are none in the area?"

"Listen you think I am a taxi service! You better be ready when I get there. You don't put gas in my car."

"No I don't put gas in your car, but I'm always lending your ass gas money." Thirty minutes later he pulls up bitching before I even got into the damn car. It is pouring rain and he sends our daughter in to call me out of the school with no hat and no umbrella. Immediately I call Zayle and tell her what the hell this fucking idiot just did knowing that the kids were just sick and at the doctor's office yesterday.

92

This pisses me the fuck off. She says nothing, which I think is so unfair since she was always rambling off about something Suzanne did and I always listened, and here I am trying to vent and she is not participating saying that she didn't want to discuss him.

All the way home he is bitching and carrying on. I'm just maintaining my composure because I know that I am going to see my baby and I hadn't seen her in about four weeks. We walked into the apartment and I called her and told her that I was on my way over to her house right now. I got the kids settled and told Darren that I would be back.

It took me about fifteen minutes to get there I couldn't believe I got there so quickly, this could be good….and it could be bad… I felt a lot safer knowing that she was right there, but now there was more of a chance that I will be running into her and Suzanne, and I guess more chances of her seeing Darren even though at this point we knew we both were living with other people but we never really had to deal with it. At least she never did….

I took a cab to her house while talking to her on the phone.

"Baby I'm here, what is your bell number?"

"Stay right there, don't come up. I'm coming down to get you.",

Now I catch an attitude. What is it now? Is it that she doesn't want me to know the fucking bell number? I hear footsteps coming down the stairs and then stop. My phone rings.

"Baby, I'm about to open the door but before I do, turn off your phone…and hold your hands out." What the hell is up with this mission impossible bullshit, I do it anyway. She opens the door while I have my hands held out and my eyes closed. She turns me around ties a scarf around my eyes, took my pocketbook off of my shoulders, and led me up the stairs.

Going up the stairs I felt a little disoriented because I was used to her old apartment. This was my first time being at the new apartment. She had just gotten the keys from the landlord and I had only seen it once before when she was considering buying it.

While I try to catch my bearings, I smelled food, seafood to be exact. I thought it was coming from one of her neighbor's apartments. We got closer, she offered to take off my coat before opening up the door, and led me inside. Once inside she hugged me and kissed me and said, "Baby, I know this is not our apartment but I hope this will make you feel a little better." and took the scarf off of my eyes. I was in total shock. There were tea light candles lit all over the entire apartment. My favorite incense was burning and slow jams were playing in the background.

She led me into the dining area where on the floor she had a blanket spread out, and on the blanket she had my favorite, seafood and coke and her favorite seafood pasta and juice. I couldn't do anything I stood there in shock and disbelief. She took my hands and led me over to the blanket and said "Baby look I even got your red velvet cake."

I couldn't say anything… I just looked at her and hugged her. She led me to the blanket and we sat down and ate our food. We talked, laughed, and made jokes with each other about me still being upset with her over the night before.

Honestly I wasn't upset anymore but I was torn between letting her know that I wasn't upset anymore or just letting go and enjoying the moment. I choose to just let it go and enjoy the moment. After the beautiful festivities I offered to help her clean the place up which is when she told me to get up and close my eyes again. Her phone rang and it was Suzanne but she hit ignore and turned to me and says, "I'm sorry baby I thought I turned my phone of also."

She then took me and told me to stand right here. I heard water running...Oh man! Zayle came back out and started to undress me. As she pulled my shirt over my head and over my arms, she turned and kissed me on my forehead and then on my lips and whispered in my ear "Baby, I love you so much, do you know that? Do you know that I would give you the world if that would make you happy?"

I went to try and answer her but she took her finger and silenced my lips. I had to laugh because we have this longstanding joke that I talk too much and never give her a chance to say anything. She led me into the bathroom where she had the shower running nice and warm how I love it. She turned me around so that my back was towards her so she could pull my hair back into a ponytail for me. She then turned me back around and led me into the shower. She lathered me up and rinsed me off, but it was so soft and gentle that it really wasn't sexual at all. I mean, oh hell yes I was turned on because I am human, but it was more of her just taking care of me.

See no one ever takes care of me. It has always been me taking care of people. I am always doing things to surprise them: friends, family, lovers. After rinsing me off she led me out of the shower and gently dried me off. She then rubbed my favorite body oil onto me and then took a big terry cloth robe and wrapped me in it and told me to stay there again. I took a seat on the toilet cover to wait for her but in the other room I could hear saying "Shit!" and "Damn," I start to laugh out loud and I cracked the bathroom door open to ask her "Babe, is everything all right?"

"You don't worry about a thing, just keep your pretty little self in there and don't move a muscle. You hear me?"

"I won't..."

I kept laughing because I kept hearing this loud ridiculous vacuum sound.

Now I'm wondering what she's vacuuming because I know she said the apartment didn't have any carpet, and I know I didn't see any on my way into the apartment. What was she up to? After hearing a barrage of shits and damns, she finally came back into the bathroom looking like she had just run a marathon. She took my hands and led me into one of the rooms. She was in the other room all this time blowing up a blow up bed....awww. She made the bed up with a sheet and also had red, white, and pink rose petals scattered all over the bed.

 In the back ground she had a CD playing that she made for me the first time that she ever told me she loved me. I remember the CD track-by-track because I played it almost every day especially when we argued.

"Baby I want to make love to you but not on a hard ass floor, you're too special for that. You deserve better than that! I ran home to get everything to make you feel comfortable, and as fucked up as it may sound I wanted memories of us making love in this new place."

Before I could say anything she took me in her arms and started to passionately kiss me.

She held me so close and so tight that I could not move even if I wanted to. She pulled the ponytail holder out of my hair because she loved to see and feel my hair on my shoulders, and laid me down on the bed. We both started to laugh because of course the bed felt very awkward. We were so used to being on regular beds, so this was one that we would laugh about in weeks to come. She started to caress me and kiss me all over my body so gently, so sweet, and savoring every kiss as if it would be her last.

I couldn't take it any more I grabbed her and pushed her head straight down to my groin area and she knew exactly what I wanted and she did it. She ate me out. She ate my pussy as if it were her last meal, slow soft and gentle.

Within no time I climaxed and we flipped over and I began to ride her. This is something that she taught me how to enjoy. Previously with any other female I slept with, it was

always you suck my pussy and that's it. No hug, no kiss, nothing and don't even think of asking me to go down on you that was a definite No. Fortunately or unfortunately, depends on how you look at it, I was lucky that females just wanted to eat me and didn't care one bit if I went down on them or not. Dahlia use to always laugh at me and ask me how the hell do these females know that I even get down like that, like I had a sign on my forehead.

I climbed on top of her and positioned myself exactly on her clit so that she could feel mine and experience the pleasure that I knew she loved. She always told me that she loved the way that I moved my body on top of hers and her eyes and body always told me that she was not lying. After we finally climaxed together, I got up and decided to give her a treat since today was going so well.

I got up and started to give her a private dance show, although I was already completely naked so I couldn't strip. I gyrated and danced as if I was on a stage and all eyes were on me. After she couldn't take it anymore she sat up and pulled me down towards her and started to kiss me. I took being on top of her to my advantage and laid her down on her back. I began to fondle her breasts and take each one gently into my mouth. This drives her absolutely insane. Then I started to work my way down, slow and hesitant because I know at any given moment she will stop me.

She's never really let me make love to her. It's hard to explain. She would make love to me and as crazy as this may sound, it made me feel that since I didn't reciprocate, I would never have to define my sexuality.

But in reality it's a little like saying I drink alcohol every chance I get and everywhere I am but I am not an alcoholic because I pour it in a glass and not drink it straight from the bottle. Both make no sense.

Although she is extremely sexual she really isn't into getting her pussy sucked. She would always tell me "Babe, I have to be in a mood," which never came. So I would always wait for her to give me some kind of signal. Surprisingly, this time she didn't stop me. I was so excited that I didn't know what to do, but I kept on going, just waiting for her to signal me to stop. In my head I'm thinking, ok any minute she is going to stop me, and I won't even have to go there. I've never done this before and never even attempted to.

I kept working my way down, and then I noticed that she slightly opened her legs as if to invite me to enter and boy did I take the invitation. I started to lick her slowly while playing with her breasts.

I found myself enjoying myself to the point where I was getting even more turned on just by eating her out, but in my head all I'm thinking is "Damn, is she enjoying this? Is it any good?" Hell, I'm no expert. Regardless I decided to listen to her body, and it was telling me that she was indeed enjoying it and it was feeling good to her.

She climaxed and as soon as she climaxed she flipped me over before I could even say a word and started to go down on me again. In between licks we're both talking and saying how much we love each other and why couldn't this be our place. Just as I was about to cum, and cum hard, we hear a loud bang and running up the stairs. We both jump up "Oh shit, what the hell was that?"

We are naked, sweaty and pussy smelling all in the air. There would be no way to explain this shit. We were both idiots just sitting there listening to hear if the door would open, butt ass naked, on a bed with my cum all over her face and hers all over mine. The dumbest person in the world would be able to figure this shit out. We're both not saying a word, just listening to hear the door open. What the hell are we both just sitting there for?

Did we want to get caught? Did we want Suzanne to walk in and catch us? I started to get dressed and she followed suit. I started to feel sad and started to cry. She walked up to me and just hugged me. She knew why I was crying without me even saying a word.

"I'm tired baby of the hiding and rushing and sneaking. Aren't you tired of it?"

She looked at me, threw a glass across the room and just hugged me tight. We both got dressed and she cleaned up the place, while I looked out of the window and wondered if I would ever look out of "our" window. Would we ever make love in "our" place?

She looked at me and simply said babe "I know", with out me even saying a word, she knew what I was feeling. This was a regular thing for us. She asked me not to go home but to go to the mall with her instead. I decided to go.

I knew tomorrow was another day and I wouldn't be able to see her for maybe a few days until they got situated and we left.

Chapter 11

W hy are these people driving as if they have nowhere to go? Shit, I am already fifteen minutes late for work. The kids are home today, since every other week there is some kind of holiday, or half a day. What do they expect working parents to do? Thank God my mother has an abundance of days that she can take off to help me, but of course I overslept this morning, and so we ended up getting a late start out of the door. Then on top of all this shit, my cell phone is off. Anyone who knows me, knows that Anaiyah Williams cannot do without her cell phone. First of all the practice gives me an allowance to pay my bill every month. It would just be nice if I could remember to pay it on time.

I finally arrive at the job and it is already hectic. All my fellow members of the practice are all ready backed up with three check-up appointments. Since it is flu season, it seems as if every single child in the borough of Manhattan was in today for their shots. All throughout the day I am calling Darren to ask him if he could go to my mom's house to relieve my mother of the children just a little earlier than usual for me. I knew I wouldn't get out of the office until at the very least 9:00 p.m. Of course; no response but that didn't surprise me.

"Hey Dr. William's there is someone here to see you," the secretary's voice came over the paging system.

"Who is it? Tell them I am with a patient but I will be right there."

I walk out of the examination room only to see Zayle standing there looking as cute as ever but sad in the eyes.

"Zaye, hi what are you doing here?"

"What, you're not glad to see me?"

"Of course I am but didn't you have a meeting with a client tonight?", I asked.

"Yes I did but it was not far from here so I decided to stop in and see you first."

"Aww babe, I'm glad you did. I am feeling so tired right now."

With that we decided to go out and get a quick bite to eat before my next patient. I told the receptionist that I would be right back and we headed for the elevator. As we were getting in to the elevator, we heard over the overhead paging system, "Dr. Williams, please pick up line eight Warren Daniels is holding."

Shit, why the hell would this bitch page me over the loud speaker and she sees me walking out with Zayle. No one at the job knew we were "together" except for my only friend Sandra and that was the same dumb bitch that just paged me with that dumb shit. Why would she do that? If I saw her with her boyfriend I wouldn't do that shit.

There was nothing to hide because truth of the matter was, she still lived with her girlfriend, and Darren was still parading in and out of my house, but I didn't keep secrets from her, and I didn't want her to think that I started now.

I know her very well and I knew that she heard that page as loud and clear as I did, and was not about to let it go just like that. Before the elevator doors could even close I hear "So who is that?"

"Huh? Oh that is just a friend."

"So, if it is just a friend why is she overhead paging you? She doesn't do that for me when I call."

"What are you talking about ZAYE, of course she does!"

" So why is he so important that she paged your ass on over head?"

"Zaye stop it ok. Let's just go and get something to eat. You know I have to go back to the office in a few minutes, so please stop."

She is walking damn near a half a mile in front of me, what is her problem? Here I am trying to figure out a way to help her ass and she is catching an attitude with me, what the hell? Suzanne is the one that emptied out her bank account not me. She is the one that owes Supreme not me.

"ZAYE!!!!!" , She kept on walking, jumped in her jeep, and sped off. You know what fuck her.

I dial Dahlia. "Dee, you would never believe what just fucking happened!"

"Oh God, what happened?"

"Ok, first off Zaye surprised me at work. As we are walking out of the office, a page comes over the over the intercom system that there is a call for me."

"Ok, Nai, what is the problem with that?"

"Dahlia, they announced Warren Daniels!"

"Oh shit Anaiyah and guess what he is in town today and may be that is why he called you at work."

"Are you serious?   Ok let me call you back my next appointment should be here."

"Naia, wait, did you ever explain your situation to him?"

"What situation, it came up at dinner that night and never came up again, so I just left it alone. I'll call you later when I get off. Love ya, bye."

"Love ya crazy ass too Naia, bye."

 I went back into the office and finished out what turned out to feel like the longest day I ever had at work. I kept calling her and got no answer. I knew I couldn't drive to the courthouse since by the time I finished what I had to do here she would be done for the day. I called her secretary and left a message that it was urgent that she returned my call and still nothing.

I even thought about calling Suzanne and asking her to have Zayle call me but decide against that.

I didn't feel like dealing with her.

Every time I spoke with her I hung up feeling like shit. She would always ask me to "speak" to my best friend and to reassure Zayle that everything would be all right.

I hated being in that position, I wanted to tell her, "Asshole she is sleeping with me," but I couldn't. I didn't call Warren back. I had to get my shit fixed first before I could call anyone.

I called her, "Baby stop acting like this. Did you speak to the guy about the money you owe him? Please call me?" Still nothing. Fuck it I'm going over there. I call Darren and tell him that I am working late and ask him to please pick up the kids for me from mom's house. Of course that was a ten minute yelling and screaming match.

"Darren, please pick up the kids from my mom's house. Please, I have to work late."

"Girl, are you mad? I don't even know what time I'm getting off myself. You always want somebody to do something for you and I can't even get sex."

"You know what Darren, I have to work ok? What does sex have to do with anything? Just please pick them up for me!"

By the time I hung up with him I got another sharp pain in my chest, this shit has been going on since the night we saw Darren in Long Island. Ok this is too much, I have to go to the doctor because I don't want to have a heart attack and these pains are coming too often. I decide to stop off at a colleague's office before I go to Zayle's house. I called her and told her that I would be right there. I got there within twenty minutes flat.

"Girl what's going on with you? Jump up here and let me check your pressure. Wow, your pressure is 160/90. Shit! Anaiyah, I need to put you on medication."

"Are you serious? I didn't even feel it except that I was getting headaches but I blew them off as migraines."
She listened to my heart and found that I had Tachycardia, which meant that my heart was beating too fast. Without hesitation she pulled a shit load of blood from my veins.

"See this is what I am afraid of, that something would be wrong". I get dressed and go over to Zayle's house, first stopping off at the pharmacy to fill my prescription.

I pull up and notice that her car is parked on the street. I walk up and ring the bell but Suzanne came down. "Hey Naia, what's up? Looking for your friend? Come on up."

"Thanks."

I walk up the stairs and enter the house and walk into the kitchen to find her washing the dishes. Suzanne looked high as usual. I walked into the kitchen and Zayle still didn't turn around to face me. "Baby, I didn't come here to argue or fight, I came to tell you that I just came from the doctor's office and I have high blood pressure and my heart is beating too fast so they put me on medication."

She looked to see where Suzanne was and grabbed me by my shirt collar, "Baby I need you to take care of yourself, but who the hell is Warren Daniels?"

"Baby he is just a friend I met threw Dahlia."

"Oh great! So Dahlia is hooking you up with people now?"

"No baby, it's not like that, I met him and we spoke on the phone a few times. He doesn't even live in New York."

As we are speaking, Suzanne enters the kitchen. I turned around to pretend that I was getting a glass of juice, walked over to the table and took a seat.

"Naia, please speak to Zayle, I think she is seeing someone else, I don't think she loves me anymore."

Zayle flew up at her, "Sue, shut your high ass up, go in the other room. Can't you see I had a long day in court, I don't need to hear this bullshit right now!"

And so it begins, Lord I am leaving. What am I to say, yes she is fucking me, and has been for the past few months now. I don't think so. Yes I feel like the devil in hell right now, with gasoline drawers, but we have more important things to discuss right now.

"Babe I was thinking about asking that same guy to lend me the money, so th3.3at you can pay Supreme back."

"Ok and then when he wants pussy, what are you gonna say then?"

"No, I will give him the papers for my jeep, it's paid off for, and you will pay it back, right?"

"Nai, of course I would, but I don't want you doing that, ok don't do it!"

"Ok, I won't."

Chapter 12

All the way home I'm trying to figure out how I am going to help her, but I am coming up with nothing, nada. The only person I know with that kind of money right now is Warren. At least it seemed as if he had that kind of money but there was only one way to find out. Question is "What was the way?" I'm not good at running game on niggas that was Dahlia's specialty. I go home and decide to call Warren to see if I can work my magic on him. I know what Zayle said but hey, I had to work my magic right? Who else would save her? Definitely not Suzanne, or was I trying to convince myself that I was the only one that could save her.

Every other girl I know, has played some nigga or the other to get what they want, shit I'm just as pretty or prettier, I'm sure I can work my charm.

"Hey baby, I heard you called me today. I'm sorry, I was in a meeting."

"Hey pretty lady, I can't talk right now, I will be in NY in the morning, clear your schedule for me ok," he said.

"Ok, Wait before you go, can I plan a surprise for you? Will you have time?"

"Go ahead. On Saturday I'm all yours. Gotta go, see you in the morning."

"Bye."

"Bye."

How the hell was this going to work? The man barely has time to even hold a conversation with me, how was I to even know if he liked me. This was crazy. I go in the kitchen to microwave some leftover food from the night before and then I call Dahlia. I needed some information on him, like whether he had a girlfriend, baby mother or mothers, like what was really his deal. She was really no help because all she kept saying was, "I don't know, all I know is that he likes you."

"Thanks Dahlia." Of course she rushed off of the phone to tend to her man company. When it came to this girl and her "dick" no one could compete. I woke up early the next morning and decided to plan a spa day for Warren. I texted him earlier that morning and found out that he would be arriving at *"JFK"* airport at 9:30 a.m. and he said I could plan anything for him after that until the evening. I called my favorite spa, and planned an entire day for him: a facial, manicure, pedicure, body scrub, and body wrap. I headed to his friends house in Queens to pick him up as soon as I got his text saying that he arrived and ready.
I pull up in front of the house and call him.

"Hey Warren, I'm outside."

"Ok, I'm coming out sexy lady"

I call Dahlia, "Hey Dee, I'm here with Warren if you need me. If Zaye or Darren happen to call you, don't answer ok?"

"No problem, I'll be at work anyway. I have a few patients."

"Cool."

With that I hung up and here comes Mr. Handsome, dressed from head to toe in my favorite designer, *"Gucci"*. If he was trying to impress me he's damn sure doing a great job.

As soon as he sat in the car, I reached in the back seat and pulled out a bottle of *"Dom Perignon"* that I had chilling from earlier for him.

"I hope you like this…"

"Damn Babe, you are a woman of class. Thank you so much!"

"That's ok, just sit back and relax."

He must've had jet lag, because he sat back and slept the entire drive from Queens to Brooklyn.

As soon as I pulled up in front of the spa I woke him up and he got up ready to fight, "Whoa cowboy, it me Anaiyah!"

"I'm sorry Nai. A guy like me has to stay on guard at all times. Where are we?"

"Look over there."

"Oh, you're going into the spa."

"No, you are."

The look on his face said it all. He was shocked. I got out of the jeep and explained to him that today was his day. I then took him inside and told him that I would return as soon as it was over. He gave me a big bear hug and I left.

I headed over to the doctor's office to see if my test results had came in.

Luckily they had come back and she informed me that I was as healthy as a horse with the exception of high blood pressure. My echocardiogram that I took to check the chambers of my heart came back clean.

The HIV test was negative and the only problem with my blood was that I had extremely low iron. She prescribed a blood pressure medication for me, called Lopressor, which would also help slow down the fast rhythm of my heart by blocking the adrenaline. God I knew my anxiety and stress would make me sick one day, I just didn't know it would manifest physically. By the time I left the doctor's office it was time to pick Warren up. When I arrived he was just finished getting dressed and was happy to see me.

"Girl, I've never had anyone do something this special for me, this was amazing, but are you trying to turn me in to a softie?"

"No, I'm not, I'm just being me"

"Well if you're just being you, you're trying to make me fall for you."

With that we turn and get into my jeep. My text messages start to go off, beep, beep, beep. I look down at my cell and it's Zayle. God damn it! She never has time for me on a Saturday, but of course with my luck she has time today. I text her back quickly, as to not draw attention to it by casually mentioning that it was my cousin.

Z- Where are you and what are you doing?

Me- Roosevelt Field Mall with my kids and aunt.

Z – Oh ok! I'm taking my mom and sister shopping in Manhattan. I have to drop my phone off at the Sprint store if you try to text or call and don't get me.

Me - Ok babe, call me when you're finished.

He was still talking while I was texting and driving.

"Hey are you ready to go home or do you want to catch a movie?", I asked.

"You said you had a day planned for me, so you tell me.", he said with a big grin.

"Ok we are going to the movies."

This guy was just making me like him more and more. Neither Zayle nor Darren ever wanted to go with me to the movies, no matter how much I begged them to go; especially not Darren because he was always too busy doing other things. Zayle, she just never wanted to go period, end of story. I figured since Zayle was on her way to Manhattan, it would be safer to go to the movies in Brooklyn, on Linden Boulevard. It was not near any malls so I was safe.

We decided to see any movie that was showing around the time that we arrived; it didn't really matter because we were playing luck of the draw. I purchased the tickets, and we bought popcorn and soda and the usual junk food moviegoers get. All the while he is commenting on how beautiful I am.

112

The movies were about to start so we headed over to the section that our movie was showing and handed in our tickets.

I stopped to use the bathroom, and hurried out because I didn't want to end up getting up half way through the movie to go pee. As I walk out into the lobby, I smell a familiar fragrance that I know all but too well. Hell no, it can't be! I turn quickly and run back into the bathroom and go into a stall only to hear two people enter the bathroom, this time with a familiar voice.

What the fuck, is that Zaye?

Warren must have thought I was in there taking a shit but I couldn't come out, I had to get confirmation but wait a minute; I'm not supposed to be here either. I climb up onto the toilet, and dial her cell phone. I had to make sure it was her. As soon as TI's song came blasting on, *"You can have whatever you like",* right away, that was her. She hit ignore, this bitch must be crazy. I hit redial, this time she didn't even let it ring, she sent me straight to voice mail, is this bitch crazy?

"OK ZAYLE WHO IS THAT CALLING YOU EVERY MINUTE !" the other woman asked.

This heifer has the nerve to be questioning her.

"Babe, relax that is just my cousin, she harassing me."

No the fuck she didn't just say I am her cousin. I had enough of this shit; I come out of the bathroom stall and walk right up on this bitch, this time dialing her, while I am walking up to her.

"So this is Sprint Zaye?" as I said that I grabbed the phone out of her hand and threw it against the mirror. The entire mirror shattered and in came Warren and two female security guards.

"Naia, what the fuck is going on?" he said as he walked into the bathroom.

"Warren, give me a minute please!!!!."

The security guards came in the bathroom and threw him out.

"Ladies, let's move it before someone gets locked up tonight!" said this big brawling guard.

The security guards come back running into the bathroom, but not before I snatch the bitch by her shirt collar. "Ask Zayle who the fuck am I? I'm not her fucking cousin, I'm her fucking woman, that's who the fuck I am!"

The security guards held onto me as tight as they could, and Zayle still wasn't saying shit.

"Well, Zayle told me she didn't have a fucking woman!"

"Well she doesn't now, cause you can fucking have her".

"Ladies you will all have to leave the movie theatre."

"Bitch, shut the fuck up", is all I could tell this brawling guard. "Let me go!"

"Miss if I let you go I have to walk you outside."

114

"Let me go!"

As soon as she let me go I approached her to do something we swore we would never do to each other but I am consumed with rage and I want blood, I am going to punch her dead in her face. I walk over to her and as I am walking over to her the girl is standing there with her hand on her hips yelling at Zaye. "Who the fuck is she Zayle?" and walks up into her face and chucks her.

Oh hell no that is my girl, is she fucking crazy, "Who the fuck are you, to put your hands on her?" I ask her as I walk over to her and drag her by her coat and throw her ass across the lobby. "If anyone is owed an explanation it's me!"

Zayle still isn't saying a word. That's when it happened. I swung my open hand at her as hard as I could but she must've expected it. Just as it was about to make contact with her face, she caught my hand. Even though she deserved it, I still felt bad because we swore to never ever lay a hand on each other no matter what. We knew once the hitting game started, it would never end. The ice would be broken on hitting and we would end up always resorting to that.

She wiped the tears from my eyes and turned to walk away. Lord I turn around and Warren is standing there, hands folded leaning up on the wall. Immediately I know I have to go. I walk up to him and hand him a hundred dollar bill. "I'm sorry Warren, I can't deal with this right now. Just please take a cab and go home".

I can hardly breathe at this point because I am crying so hard my eyes are swelling. She turns around when she gets to the door, sees me standing there talking to him, and turns back. Shit.

We're both wrong, but I was doing this for a purpose. What was she doing this for? She walks over to us, sticks her hand out and says, "Hi, I'm Zayle, Naia's lover, and you are?"

He was so shocked all he could say was "Hi, I'm Warren, Naia's friend."

She continues, "Well, I just fucked up and I'm sure I've lost her for good. Take care of her ok". Then she takes me, grabs my face and kisses me in front of him.

She walks off, and I turn to Warren to tell him to go ahead. As I'm walking off he stops me. "Come on lets go, I'll drive you home"

"Are you sure? "

"Come on."

We walk to my car, and I get into the passenger side while he drives me home. He didn't say a word and I was glad. I never did explain to him my situation because we never continued the conversation from the night we had dinner.

All the way there we drove in complete silence. We pulled into the drive way and he parked. I didn't even move to come out of the jeep. He walked around to my side and opened my door; he took my hand and led me out of the car.

As we entered my apartment he walked in behind me. I turned to tell him he could go now but to my surprise he said that I shouldn't be alone right now and that he doesn't really understand what is going on, but when I was ready I could explain it all to him. Is this man for real?

116

Most men would have started with the gay jokes and probably have cursed me out and left me at the theatre, much less drive me home and say I don't need to be alone. I told him he could have a seat while I went into my room and called Dahlia.

"Dee, its me I need to talk to you."

"What's wrong, are you crying? What the hell happened?" she continued, "Did Warren do something to you?"

"No, it's Zayle, I caught her with another woman at the movies."

"What?!"

"Where's Warren? Where was he when all this went down?"

"He's in the living room, he brought me home."

"What? Are you serious? Did he know about her?"

"No I never told him about her, all I said was that I was dealing with a woman, but never explained."

Before I could go any further, he knocked on the bathroom door. "Are you ok? Come out."

"Listen Dee, let me call you back, ok? Let me go talk to him".

"Ok, call me back. I'm here if you need me, ok? I love you, call me."

"I love you too, I will."

"Naia, there is no need for you to be hiding in the bathroom, you told me you were in a relationship with a woman, talk to me. What's going on?" Warren asked.

I walked in front of him and went to the couch and took a seat. I couldn't stop crying. After all this time and everything we've been through, how could she do this to me? I mean, I knew about Suzanne, she was there before me, but it's been two years and I haven't slept with Darren, Warren or anyone except her, how could she?

"Talk to me, come sit here." he said as he motioned for me to sit beside him.

"What is there to say, huh? I'm a fool, an asshole, I'm in love with someone who isn't in love with me!"

He looked at me as if he understood. But did he really? How could he?

"Go, on, and why would you say you're a fool?"

"It's a WOMAN! Ok, did you not see that I'm being played by a woman!"

"Ok but babe, talk to me."

"Warren, what am I to say, huh?"

Through my tears, I explained as best I could that she was my best friend and I fell in love with her.

"We have been together now two years, and she lives with her woman still. She has been the only person that I have been sleeping with for the last two years. I have been sticking with her, through all her promises to be with me fully, to move out and live with me, and in the midst of all these promises they bought a condo, and I am still here waiting on her to decide to be with me. I'm a fool huh? I really believed that there was no one else." Why would she need anyone else? We sleep together at least three times a week. I don't even know when we actually officially started to date, it just happened.

He took my hands and drew me into his chest, and held me while I cried.

Chapter 13

I was so exhausted from crying that I fell asleep on his chest. A cramp in my legs awoke me out of my sleep and caused me to startle him, except his reaction was to hold me tighter. He then got up and led me into my bedroom, and laid me down on the bed. I glanced at the clock and it's already 2:30 a.m. I knew he should leave but I didn't want to be alone. He laid at the foot of the bed and started to rub my feet. I let him continue because it felt so damn good. My heart was shaking but was there something to stop this pain? Hell no! Is this what people mean when they say they have a broken heart? I can literally feel the pain piercing my chest. Then my cell phone rings, it was Zaye.

I really shouldn't answer, but of course I did.

"Hello."

"Yeah, so you fucked him huh? Well I'm about to suck that same girls pussy that you saw me with," she screamed sounding wasted. There was a lot of noise in the background and all I heard was a girl tell her to hang up the phone.

"FUCK YOU ZAYLE!!!!", I screamed into the phone before, I threw it across the room. I started to cry again.

"Anaiyah, why are you letting this girl, get to you? She will be right back here."

I sat up, grabbed him and pulled him closer. Fuck it maybe I should sleep with him. The only dick I've been getting and wanting is her's, so maybe I should go ahead and sleep with him. Shit, she's about to suck some girl's pussy right? Plus she had the nerve to call me and tell me! Fuck her! Maybe this whole girl thing is not for me anyway. She is the only woman I've been with but that doesn't make me a lesbian...does it?

I don't look at women and lust after them. Maybe it was just something about her; the fact that I could just be myself, no hang-ups, just myself. I pull him on top of me but I have all of my clothes on still. Of course him being a man, he got hard instantly. He felt as if he had a big dick because it was surely sticking out of his pants. He tried to kiss me but I turned my head. I was too used to kissing her.

I didn't even kiss Darren; he didn't even get a kiss when we were still living in the same house, so Warren wasn't about to get one either. He starts to feel me up and inside I'm cringing. I feel so disgusted but fuck it why not. He starts to unbutton my blouse, pulling my bra down and at the same time running his fingers over my breasts while cupping my breasts with his hands. Oh God, I feel nasty but let me just continue. I need to forget Zayle Ford and maybe this will help me break the spell that she has over me.

He starts to pull my pants down and as I was about to stop him. A mental picture of Zayle eating another woman out flashed into my head and I let him continue. He starts to comment on how beautiful my tattoos are which didn't make it any better, because they were for her. We went together to get them and they represented her. At this very moment the tattoo saying Pain is love, Love is pain is becoming very real. He starts to unzip his pants and pulls out his dick.

Oh god I start to cry silently, but he hears me sniffle. I push him up off of me.

"I can't do this just because she is being an asshole. I can't do this"….

"Wait a minute, I didn't come onto you; you came onto me. Look, I have a condom." and he takes one hand and rolls it on.

"Warren, I'm sorry. I'm sorry that I led you on, but I can't do this."

"What the fuck you mean you can't do this? I didn't come here to fuck you but you led me on!"

He then starts to force my legs open. Oh shit what have I gotten myself into? Oh God! Someone help me. I start to panic now because this is not the same man that I thought was so kind and gentle. My phone is nowhere near me because I threw it across the room. He takes his knee and forces my legs open while he is pinning my hands down with his forearms. I'm really crying hard now while trying to close my legs, but he is so much stronger than me I can't. My legs start to tremble from me straining the muscles.

"Please Warren, I beg you, please don't do this."

"So let me ask you a question, is she the only person you've been sleeping with for two years?"

"Yes."

"No dick, just her sucking your pussy?"

"Yes."

"What about toys? Don't y'all use toys? I have a sister who's a carpet licker and I know y'all bitches are freaks. Don't y'all use dildo's, strap-on's, and all that freaky shit?" I didn't answer him. He continues, "You bring me to the fucking movies and embarrass me. I'm sure people thought I was a fucking punk."

"'Warren, please, I'm sorry, please don't do this."

"Fuck you Naia, all this? You're fine as hell, and you're running down a woman? I spent my fucking money on you. I thought you were just getting your pussy sucked every now and again, I didn't know that y'all were in a relationship."

"Warren, you're hurting me, please get off of me."

While still pinning me down, he takes his other hand to stop my alarm clock. It was set to wake me up at 4:30 a.m. in the morning since I had to cover at the office. He then opened the drawer on my side table to throw it in, and in doing that he saw Zayle's dildo.

"Oh, so here it is huh!! This is what y'all use?"

He takes it out and starts to laugh at it. "My dick is bigger than this plastic shit! I could fuck you better any day." he tells me.

"Warren, please. I get the point and I am sorry. I should not have led you on. Ok, I was wrong and I apologize."

He then takes the dildo and shoves it with all his might into my dry vagina, OH MY GOD ! I can't even scream because the pain was unbearable. It felt as if he took a spiked brush and shoved it into me. My vagina felt as if it were on fire and he pulled it out and shoved it in at least ten times making me feel as if I was going to die. Did I really deserve this God? What did I do? He took the dildo and flung it across the room.

"You stupid bitch! Running down some fucking dyke, when you could have a real man like me". "FUCK YOU!!" was the last thing I heard as he slammed my room door.

I lay there in so much pain. Besides the fact that I was only sleeping with her, we didn't even use the dildo in months so my vagina had in fact, for lack of a better word, closed up. Oh God, what am I going to do? Who can I call? I need Zayle.

I begin to call her, amazingly she answered. "Zayle, please I need you. I need you right now, please come over!"

"Naia, I hurt you, you don't need me. Go ahead and find someone else to make you happy. Ok?"

"Zayle you don't understand, please, I've been raped!"

"WHAT ? YO WHERE THE FUCK ARE YOU RIGHT NOW?"

"I'm home baby, please I need you."

She clicked the phone in my ears. It seemed as if she was standing outside of my door, because the next thing I knew I heard my door burst open with a bunch of commotion.

"YO WHAT THE FUCK YOU SAID NAIA?"

I couldn't even move off of the bed because my vagina was hurting me so fucking bad. She came over to me on the bed and asked me again… "Baby what happened?"

When she looked beside me she saw the dildo on the bed,

"WHAT THE FUCK?"

I started to cry even harder. She took me up off of the bed and led me into the bathroom. I sunk to the floor in the shower. She said she would be right back because she left her "boys" in the living room. She came back into the room, dried me off and gave me my sweat suit to put on.

"Tell me what happened," she asked.

I was too embarrassed; to say but I could not lie to her so I told her the truth. From beginning to end.

"I was going to try and use my charm on him to get the money for you to repay the guy that was planning to black mail you. That was the reason that I took him to the movies. I never planned to sleep with him, but I trusted him because he was Dahlia's friend." I explained.

"He's Dahlia's friend? Let's go!"

"Where are we going?"

"I said LETS GO!!!"

I got up and followed behind her. As we entered my living room I saw ten men sitting in my living room. One of them is the guy that she owed money to and then I knew this night was not going to end on a peaceful note. I recognized her cousin Supreme, who had just come out of jail for murder and this man was not wrapped too tight in the head department.

He pulled out a 9mm handgun and said, "Let's do this!"

Oh my God.

She turns to me and says, "Baby, all you have to do is tell me one thing. Did you want him? Were you attracted to him at all? Better yet, did you say stop?"

"Baby I told you the truth. I never wanted him, I was just feeling confused, and I did tell him stop."
"That's all I need to know, let's go."

We all pile into separate cars and head over to Dahlia's house. Zayle turned to me and told me to call Dee and tell her to leave her house now. I call her, "Dahlia, leave your house now."

"Naia, what?"

"Leave your house right now, I'll explain later. Please just trust me."

"Ok, I'm walking out now."

Ten minutes later we pull up in front of her house. Zayle looks at me and asks me if I'm ok.

"Go up and ring the doorbell," she commands. As I approached the door, all of the guys hid behind the hedges. I started to sweat in a panic. I'm ringing the doorbell and there is no answer. In a way I was kind of hoping that he wasn't there or that he wouldn't answer the door, not because I didn't want him to get what he deserved, but because I didn't want anyone's blood on my hands. Also I didn't want Zayle to mess up her career because of me.

I knocked again, and he came to the door "Who is it?" as he was asking the question, he opened the door. The last thing Zayle said to me before I knocked on the door was that I was to make sure that it was him, and to give her a signal by putting my hand up in the air. She was standing right behind me closest to the door. So she heard when he said to me "What's the matter Naia? I opened up your pussy now you want the real thing?"

I spit straight in his eye and he raised his hand to slap me. The next thing I knew Zayle grabbed me swung me around and threw me in the bushes. Two of the guys came charging at him with a battle rammer that the police use to break down doors. They rammed it straight into his chest and he didn't know what hit him. As quickly as they hit him with the charger, another guy tasered him, and then they called me into the house.

Afterwards they sat him on a chair. Zayle walked up to him, but as she walked up to him he tried to get up out of his seat, so they tasered him again and Zayle gun butt him. The blood splattered across the room. He went to spit at her and she slapped him right in his mouth with the butt of the gun and his lips instantly swelled to the size of mangos.

"So, you think you're a big man. Huh?" Zayle, slapped him again with the gun.

As he went to answer her she slapped him again with the gun and then she pulled me in front of him.

"First thing first, not only is this my woman but she is a lady. Who the fuck you think you are? You think taking pussy makes you a man?" she said all of this while bending down looking him straight into his eyes.

"Look I'm talking to you man to man because you know what, having a dick does not make you a man, Nigga!, I'm a bigger man than you will ever be." She then gave me the car keys and told me to leave the house right now, walked me out to the door, "Wait for me at your house."

I did as she said and left the house. As I left the house, Supreme turned to Zayle and told her to leave the house also. He pulled her to the side to tell her that he loved her and that she was his blood and that he would take care of it. By the time I got to the corner, she called me "Baby, I'm right behind you. Keep driving to the house."

"Baby, do we have to go back to the house, can we go to a hotel?"

"Ok, I understand. Drive to the hotel, I'm behind you."

Chapter 14

When we get to the *"Marriott"* we check in and immediately went up to the room. I went into the shower again because I felt so nasty. I called in sick from work and the kids were still at my mom's house, so I called her and told her that I had an emergency at work and would have to cover one of the doctor's shift. I called Darren and blocked my number because I knew he wouldn't answer otherwise. I told him the same exact thing about the emergency at work, and to please go over to my mom's house in the morning and take the kids to school.

When I came out of the shower, I asked Zayle if she could please call out from work in the morning and stay with me. The clock read 6:30 am and, it seemed like this night would never end.

She told me to come lay down and get some sleep. " Naia just relax. I'll call out sick in the morning," Zayle promised.

I fell asleep as soon as my head hit the pillow. I didn't even call to find out where Dahlia was, or if she was ok, but I was assuming that she was with her man. I would call her when I woke up later. While I was asleep Supreme called Zaye and told her to come downstairs, he had something to show her. She didn't wake me, I just heard the door slam but I was too tired to get up to look. Zayle went downstairs and got into Supremes car.

He handed her an envelope and told her to look in it. When she looked in the envelope there was fifty thousand dollars.

"Take twenty- five and pay off the guy, and keep twenty- five for yourself," he said.

Zayle was in shock and didn't even know what to say. "How the hell? Where did you get this?"

Supreme then handed her another envelope with pictures printed off of a computer with a list of email addresses out of his email. The pictures were of Warren holding guns, money, and drugs. They took his list of drug contacts, their phone numbers, bank account numbers, and even a list of suppliers, that were written in code, but they made him decode it. They even took his cell phone, along with signing onto his sprint account and printed out the phone number list. The deal cincher was a picture of Warren getting fucked in the ass by a man.

"Damn Preme, that's why I couldn't get in contact with you for the entire day, you guys were really busy. Huh?"

"Cuz, now he knows what it feels like to be forced to have sex when you say no. I bet he will respect the word from now on."

Zayle sat there in disbelief, mouth wide open in shock. "Cuz you really did this for me?"

Cuz listen, you're my blood, and I'd do anything for you. You love that girl, so I love her too. We also drove Warren to the train station and told him to take his ass back to Miami and to never come back to New York. We promised that if he did we would not only circulate the picture, we would call all of his contacts and give the information to the cops.

He could never go to the police either because he definitely had too much to lose. Plus I would have a rape case against him."

Zayle handed her back twenty- five thousand dollars and asked him to give it to Mack for her and let him know that they were now even, closed the door and came back upstairs. When she walked into the hotel room my phone was ringing, it was Dahlia. She answered the phone since I was dead asleep.

"Hello."

"Hi, Dahlia, what's up?"

"Zaye, what's going on?"

"Listen hire a cleaning service to clean up your house."

"Zaye, what happened? Is Naia ok? Why is my house a mess? Where is Warren?"

"Dee, let Nai, explain what happened all I can say is he violated her."

"WHAT?!" and she started to cry, "I'm coming over there now!"

"Nah, we're not at the house, but I'll tell her to call you when she wakes up."

All I heard was the theme song for *"Oprah"*, and when my eyes opened, it was 4:00 p.m. Zaye was still sleeping but as soon as she felt me shift, she sat up. "Babe, are you ok?"

"Do you need anything?"

"No, I'm fine, just a little hungry," and I started to cry again. She held me close to her and started to cry. "Baby, I'm to blame. If you didn't try to help me, and I wasn't being an asshole hanging out with another woman, this would not have happened."

"No if I didn't lead him on, he would not have thought I wanted him. Babe I was just playing a game with him."

"Naia let's not speak about it right now ok, just get some rest. Dahlia called you and I told her you would call her when you woke up."

I didn't know what else to say. I just placed my head in her lap and started to cry. What was I going to do with my whole situation? Did I love her so much that I was now making bad judgments and jeopardizing my life? But you know what, how was I to know that he was a predator?

While I laid there running everything through my mind and trying to make sense of it, she stood up, took a deep breath, and bent down on one knee, took both of my hands in hers and asked me. "Will you marry me? I know it's not legal in New York, but we can file domestic partnership papers."
She continued, "I'm planning to move out from Suzanne ASAP! Just please say yes, I love you."

I said yes.

Chapter 15

wo months went by and my patient load increased daily by four patients at the very least. The steady increase was the very thing that I needed if I were to make partner. I haven't made partner as yet but it is definitely looking very promising. Just last week I had a meeting with the senior doctors who informed me that if my patient load kept increasing at this rate, I was a shoe in for partner.

I have been in therapy with an associate of Dahlia's. I am ok now, I will never forget it, but I have realized that it wasn't my fault, no matter what I did; and even though he didn't physically penetrate me with his penis he still violated me. I was still raped. Rape is when you say "NO".

I never told Darren what happened to me because honestly, it would not have fazed him. All he really cared about was himself and what I could do for him. Just last month I had to co- sign on his condo for him even though he has never done anything for me, but I still helped him. It was either that, or have him move back in with me, and that was a no-no.

After doing my own investigation, I found out that his girlfriend in Long Island threw him out and got a restraining order on him. Simply put God doesn't like ugly and to prove that he isn't too fond of the pretty she took him to court for child support. Last I checked they were still waiting on the blood test results to find out if the child was his.

Now I'm not a hater but it would truly be hilarious if the child was not his. He left me with two children that he definitely knew was his for a woman and child that were uncertain.

Zayle has been winning her cases left and right. I was not surprised at all when she called me up and invited me to go to dinner with her to celebrate the verdict on a trial that had been going on for the past three months and her client won.

"Babe, I won the case! I'll pick you up from work and we will go celebrate."

All I replied was that I would be ready. She picked me up at eight o 'clock on the dot. My blood pressure had finally leveled out and I could happily eat anything that I wanted.
As I entered her jeep I gave her a big hug and a kiss because I was so proud of her. Since the incident with Warren she has not left my side once. I don't know what she told Suzanne and I really did not care. All I knew was that she was there for me.

She seemed to be very serious about to the whole city hall thing, because every single day she would mention it to me. She sized my ring finger, and even took me to her mother's house to tell her mother and family. There was one problem though she still lived with Suzanne

She even wanted us to have a baby, but that was another situation and we discussed all the options. There weren't many besides the conventional one. I had a lot of doctor friends and one just happened to be married to a doctor, which practiced reproductive medicine. The entire procedure can easily cost up to twenty thousand dollars.

The blessing was that Dr. MacIntire's wife had just given birth to their baby, and although the my practice didn't accept insurance we offered each other professional courtesy and agreed to accept each other's insurance coverage. I still had to pay out of pocket for the drugs.

The first drug I tried was Clomid. I was happy that this was the first drug since it was a pill and all I had to do was take it on the first day of my period. It helps to increase the amount of eggs that I released when I ovulated.

We agreed to use her brother Ian as the sperm donor. Ian came to my office to give his blood and I sent it to Dr. MacIntire's office to screen for STD's and HIV. We even sent for genealogy testing and everything was negative so it was a go.

"Baby are you serious about this baby thing? My period just finished and I did the first round of Clomid."

She stopped the car and turned to me. I knew when she was being genuine, and this was a genuine moment. She actually started to cry.

"Love, I have never been more serious about anything in my entire life! Let's do this." She continued. "I just don't want to know anything about the process with Ian, just surprise me".

We go to dinner and the restaurant is beautiful. As we are sitting there eating our dinner, the Matre D comes over to me and says, "Excuse me are you Dr. Williams?"

"Yes I am."

"There is a call at the front desk for you."

"For me? Who the hell would be calling me now, no one even knows that I am here." I get up and go to the Matre D's desk and answer the telephone. "Hello."

There was no one on the other end. I frustratingly hung up the telephone and headed back to the table.

Oh my God, Zayle's entire family plus Dahlia and a few of our friends were there.

"What is this?"

Zayle stood up and met me as I approached the dinner table.

"I told you that I loved you and I want everyone to know and see how much I love you. You complete me. You make me feel as if there is nothing that I can not do. The only thing left in this world, that I need or want is to have you by my side for the rest of my life."

Everyone stood there in awe with tears in their eyes. For a moment we all forgot the craziest thing …Zayle still lived with Suzanne. As a matter of fact, during the speech Suzanne called. I knew it was her because I knew her ring tone but I was not going to let that ruin my night. She reached over and handed me a black ring box. I'm feeling very nervous to open the box, especially since everyone was standing there.

The only person that was missing was my mother, which was expected because she already voiced her opinion on how she felt about me being with a woman, and that she would not accept it in any way shape or form, which I couldn't understand.

Shouldn't the most important thing be that I am happy, does it really matter whether I'm with a male or female.

I opened the box and the ring was beautiful. It was exactly what I always said that I would want if I were to get an engagement ring. The ring had to be at least two carrots square in shape with an eternity band.

Everyone started with the ooh's and awe's and I just sat there crying. Dahlia jumped up and gave a speech that embarrassed me but hey everyone there knew Dee enough that when she had a drink just let her be. Just as I was about to respond my pager went off which meant I had to leave. I was on call tonight. I stood up to thank everyone and reminded Zaye that I didn't drive so she would have to take me back to the office.

It took about twenty minutes for everyone to get into their cars and leave the parking lot. As soon as her mom left I turned to her and gave her the biggest hug I think I've ever given her. "Are you serious? Are you sure this is what you want to do? What about Suzanne?"

She looked at me very seriously, "I told Suzanne it was over and that she has to move out."

"Zaye, you've said that before, are you certain this time?"
She turned off the car and turned around completely to me in the car. "No babe, are you sure this is what you want to do? Are you sure you can handle your mother disowning you, and handle being committed to me on a full time basis? No more sneaking around, just you, me and the kids?"

"Yes."

With that we started back the car and drove home.

As soon as we got to my house, her phone starts to ring off the hook. It's Suzanne and she is telling Zaye that if she does not come home right now, she is going to burn all of her clothes. "It is ok to just go home and take care of what you have to take care of. This will all be over soon enough."

I quickly turn and remind her that I am ovulating and ask her what she wants me to do.

"Get pregnant, just no dick!"

We both laugh, I give her a kiss close my door and go inside.

I called back the patient to see what was wrong and if they wanted to meet me at the hospital.

Chapter 16

walk in my house and my answering machine light is blinking. I didn't even bother to hit play. I have too much to think about right now. I pour a glass of wine, and lay across my bed. Am I really ready to have another baby?

I get up and open the safe to read over the legal papers that Zayle drew up for Ian to sign, relinquishing all paternal rights to the child on both our ends. Basically it stated that he would never try to get legal custody of the child ever or interfere with how we raise the baby. We also included that he would never have any financial obligations to the child except in the exception that the child needed him somehow medically then he would step up.

Zayle drew up the papers months ago and Ian had his personal lawyer go over the fine details and all agreed that it was suitable. We covered every single detail down to the decision that the baby would know that he was the sperm donor but we decided to just let that one play out. It wouldn't be easy explaining to a child that your uncle is also your father and your aunt is your parent. There are no how-to books on this subject. He did say that if it was ok with us, he would participate in anything we wanted him to, so at least that was covered. Then there was money.

She knew how I felt about not having enough money, especially since I went through both my previous pregnancies worrying about money, and where things would come from. Darren was there but he was very stingy with money and only spent it or did things when he wanted.

He bought our daughter's dresser about six months after she was born. That is not my style. I like to have shit ready and prepared. When I asked her if she was monetarily ready, she said not to worry. See I didn't know that she had gotten money from the whole Warren thing and had twenty –five thousand left over.

I call Dahlia. "Dee We are gonna do it!"

"Bitch, I know! I was there and I saw the rock on your hand." She said while cracking up, "If that's the case I need to get me a girlfriend too shit."

"No ass wipe, were gonna get pregnant"

'Ok, Naia, are you sure? It's one thing to get married but now you're talking about bringing a child into this, not to mention, SUZANNE." She continued, "Did you ever stop to think about how much you and Zayle go back and forth. In two years how many times have y'all fought?"

"And got right back together." I interjected.

"True indeed, but still. Ok you guys are engaged, but there is still SUZANNE. She's been leaving Suzanne since you guys started this affair."

"Ok Dee, your right, but she said to go ahead and do it. I trust her", I guess I really just wanted Dahlia to confirm that

I wasn't really crazy. I knew that what I was about to do was definitely borderline insanity, but if she didn't say that I was crazy, at least I had one person on my side, plus she is a psychologist so maybe just maybe I am not as insane as I think I am. So I am going to do it.

I jump in my car and head to the drug store to purchase an ovulation kit just to make sure that the twinge that I am feeling in my stomach is indeed because I am ovulating. It actually hurts but the doctor explained to me that the pain is indeed because of the amount of eggs that I am releasing. He explained that there was a high chance of multiple fetuses but when we discussed it in his office Zayle still agreed to do it.

 I walked into the drugstore, purchased the kit and headed back to the car. Once in the car, I call Ian. "Ian it's time. Are you busy? Can I come get the stuff now?"

"I like how you calling my little men stuff!" he said while laughing but told me to come on over.

The drive to his house was not long, and once I got there he quickly opened the door and ran back into the room. "I'm working on your stuff now!" he yelled as he ran back into his room and closed the door.

"Wait!" I ran to the door and passed him a sterile cup, "put it in there please, and bring it right out to me."

Within five minutes, he came out. "Well damn Ian, I feel sorry for your girl. That was less than five minutes."

"Girl, please, I threw in a porno tape right after you called me and went to work. Ask my girl I don't play games! I can work it."

"Ok, can't chit chat right now I need your room get out!"
He started to laugh and walked out, "Go ahead! First my
guys, now my room, I tell you. Women…"
I locked the door, and called Zayle.

I didn't get her but I left her a message. "Baby, I'm by Ian's.
I bought the ovulation kit and I am ovulating. I am going to
do it now. Ok? Call me when you get this message. Love
you."

I went in my bag and took out the sterile syringe that I
brought from work. Dr. MacIntire and I agreed that I would
just use the syringe to inject the sperm into my vagina, of
course without the needle part. Shit women have used turkey
basters, at least I was being sterile. That would save us a
load of money also. I removed my under wear and inserted
the syringe into the cup and drew up the sperm into it. All I
needed was one shot if this was going to work, anyway.

Now it was time for the acrobatic part. I layed on my back,
spread my legs open, took one hand to open my labia,
inserted the syringe and pushed down on the lever. Presto
I'm done.

Now I have to lay here for at least thirty minutes with my ass
propped up on pillows. I put my clothes back on and prop
my ass up. Let's see what happens.

I yell for Ian to come back into the room and keep me
company. He is so sweet and he holds my hand. He tells me
that he hopes that Zayle and I get what we wish for, and that
he loves us. He handed me back the legal documents signed
and I left.

I just wish Zayle were here.

Chapter 17

Shit! Its 7:30 a.m. and I've overslept again. They are going to surely write my ass up at work. This is the fourth time this week I am late. Thank God my mother kept the kids for me last night. I jump into the shower. Damn it I need to stop for gas. The phone won't stop ringing but I can't stop to answer it now. My ass is going be caught up in the traffic on the *"FDR"*.

I run out the door wet hair and all. My cell won't stop ringing but I don't recognize the number so I just let it ring. Just as I am going over the bridge Dahlia calls.

"Hey D, was up, I'm running late."

"Hey girl, Zayle is trying to reach you. She's been calling you all morning."

"No she hasn't. From where? Her number never came up."

"She's out of town. She flew to Washington D.C. early this morning she said, call her at 202-555-1616 room 453."

"Ok thanks, I'll call her now and I'll call you back."

I call her immediately.

"Thanks for calling the *Marriott*, how may I help you?"

"Hi, Room 453 please?"

"Sure."

The phone rang three times.

"Hello."

"Hi babe, you've been calling me? I'm sorry, I didn't recognize the number. When did you leave?"

"Babe, I've been calling you all morning, I left early 3:30 a.m."

"I'm sorry babe, I didn't hear the phone. I didn't know. When are you coming home?"

"I'll be home in two days, why are you late?"

I explained to her that even though I went to bed early, I just couldn't wake up. "Baby, I think my iron is low again, I'm gonna pull my blood when I go to work, and test it."

"Babe, do you think?" she didn't get to finish her sentence because my job was beeping in on the other line.

"Baby hold on, it's my job."

Just as I thought, it was the senior doctor on the other end asking me if I planned to grace him with my presence today. Shit. I apologized profusely, and told him that I was just looking for a park, and would be in right away. By the time I went to click over, she already hung up. I didn't have time to call her back because I needed to get in there and see a few patients. As soon as I got in I had one of the nurses pull my blood and do a CBC to see my blood count and check if my iron was low again. That would explain why I've been feeling so sluggish and tired. I can't ever seem to get enough sleep, ever.

144

The first patient I saw was a five-year-old female with the stomach virus. I pulled the door open and stepped in.

"Hi Nancy, I'm Dr. Williams how are you feeling?" Her answer was a violent hurl all over my feet. Oh God, yuk.

The running joke with all my friends and the doctors in the office was that I was the only doctor who would throw up at the sight or sound of vomit. This had been proven every single time a child threw up at the office and I was next. I buzzed for a nurse to come in and help me clean up and as soon as she came in, whoops it was my turn. I high-tailed my ass into the bathroom and hurled until there was nothing left. I begged the nurse to tell Dr. Reem to finish with the patient for me. My cell phone went off again, it was Dahlia.

"Hey, what's up, I'm in the bathroom throwing up"

"Naia, are you sure your not pregnant?"

"Oh shit !, Dee, I didn't even think about that. Was it a month already?"

"Naia, you better, check it out."

"Ok, on my way home I'll pick up a test. You know what's crazy, I hadn't even thought about it."

All day I threw up, but I convinced myself that I had the stomach virus, and munched on dry crackers. The day flew by, and I called Zayle leaving her several messages to call me, but I still didn't hear anything from her by the time I was on my way home. I didn't want to leave her a message, saying hey babe, I think I'm pregnant. On the drive home, I drove by her house. I really didn't know why but I guess it was a force of habit.

All the lights were out so I kept on going until I got to my house. Shit I forgot to get the pregnancy test. It was too late now; I'll get it in the morning.

I continued to call Zayle's room. "Baby, call me", was the message I left about a thousand times.

My doorbell starts to ring. I ignored it until the person decided to keep their finger on it.

"Who the hell is it?"

"It's Darren, open the door!'

"Negro, who do you really think your yelling at? What is it?"

"Listen, I just came from your mother's house and the kids told me mommy has a pretty diamond ring."

"Yes and how the fuck is that any of your business?"

"Well I'm here to tell you if you think that you are gonna raise my kids in a gay household, you have another fucking thing coming to you!"

"Darren, get the fuck out my house! When you learn to be a father, you can talk shit then. Get out!" As I was screaming that at him, I started to throw up and I made no attempt to turn my head, I made sure it splashed on him. Asshole.

As he turned to walk out the door he yelled at me "BITCH!" And I answered him "LIKE YOUR MOTHER!"

Flashed him my engagement ring and slammed the door closed.

I immediately called Zayle's cell phone and as usual straight to voicemail, "Baby call me it's important. Darren is threatening me about marrying you, and having the kids live with us. Call me ok."

Then I called Dahlia.

"Girl Darren just came over here flipping out about me and Zayle and the kids".

"What? Are you serious? What did you say?"

"I threw up on him."

"You what?" she said as she started laughing hysterically.

I cut the conversation short and went to sleep. I wasn't feeling well and I had a feeling this virus was gonna kick my ass.

This time I heard the alarm go off, and it was accompanied by my cell phone ringing. It was Dahlia. I swear sometimes I felt as if she were my girlfriend. "Morning babe, I'm up."

"Open your door, I want to know if I am going to be an auntie"

I got up and went to open the door. There she was standing there with a "*Duane Reade* " bag in her hand.

"It has two sticks Dr. Williams, in case you miss the stick", she said while laughing."

I snatched the bag out her hands and ran to the bathroom because I was already dying to pee. I could hear her clinkering around in the kitchen yelling for me to hurry up as I sat down to pee.

I started to brush my teeth and wonder when my last period was. It wasn't late yet although I really didn't know, since I was only sleeping with Zayle and I had no reason to keep track of my period anymore. It came whenever it wanted to.

By the time I finished rinsing out my mouth, it was time to look at the stick, I'm feeling scared.

"Dee, Come in here please."

"What is it? Yes, or no?"

"I didn't look, we'll look together."

I closed my eyes and felt for it on the sink.

"Naia how the hell do you expect to see the results if your eyes are closed? Dummy, give me that", she said as she snatched the stick out of my hand.

She starts to scream, "YOU'RE A MOMMY !! YOU'RE A MOMMY !!!

I start to scream too, "ARE YOU SERIOUS? ARE YOU FUCKING SERIOUS?"

I take the test stick out of her hands and as soon as I look on it the line is pink as hell. I start to cry.

"Naia why are you crying? Isn't this what you wanted?"

"Yes."

In my heart I am feeling so terrified. Wow I'm gonna be a mom again. I ask her to call Zayle for me from my home phone, while I call the doctor to let him know.

Zayle answered and she handed me the phone, "Baby I need to speak to you. What time will you be home tonight, it's important?"

"Baby, I have a meeting tomorrow morning."

"Zayle tomorrow is Saturday, are you serious?"

"Yeah baby, but let me call you back in a few ok, I am going in to a meeting with a client right now ok, I love you."

"Love you too."

As soon as I hung up the phone, I heard the doctor say,

"Hello?"

"Hi Jim, its Naia Williams."

"Hey Doc, what's up? Hey thanks for giving my daughter the flu shot."

"No problem... Jim I'm pregnant"

"Congratulations, did you do a urine test, or a blood test?"

"A home urine test."

"Well come in this morning so that I can confirm it with a sonogram. I'll tell the secretary to expect you, say thirty minutes?"

"Ok, I'm on my way."

Thank God I was off today. I asked Dahlia if she had any patients scheduled for this morning and asked her to please follow me. As usual my ride or die best friend for life did not even hesitate. I got dressed and we headed over there.

All the way there I am feeling scared, excited, and happy all at the same time. I really didn't even expect my little implantation experiment to really work, especially not on the first try. I thought we would at least have to try four times before it really happened. I think I was also kind of hoping that it would take that long in case I changed my mind.

We enter the doctor's, office, which was filled with expectant women all advanced in their pregnancies. I started to picture myself looking like them and feeling this little person inside of me again. As soon as the secretary saw me she escorted me into an examination room. This was one of the moments that being a doctor paid off, not having to sit there in a waiting room all day just waiting for my name to be called.

I asked Dahlia to come in with me because I really didn't want to be alone for this. The doctor came in and explained to me that he would do a vaginal sonogram, because the fetus was so small.

I laid back and held Dahlia's hand while the doctor lubed up the part that goes inside my vagina and slipped it in. He turned the screen to me and confirms, "There goes your baby."

I gasped "oh my God," Dahlia starts to cry and we both start to cry. God I wish Zayle was here right now. Our baby is beautiful.

He gives me a picture of my baby and my prescription for my prenatal vitamins, and we left the office.

"Dahlia, we're heading to Washington D.C. We're going to surprise Zayle."

Chapter 18

e hit the road and head for Washington D.C. I really don't know what Dahlia's use was because she slept the entire three and a half hours that it took me to get there. I planned to surprise Zayle so I didn't call her to tell her I was heading down there. I had family in Maryland so this was a trip that I made a few times and knew my way around. I called the hotel to get the exact address and headed straight there. Before I left I stopped to pick up her favorite drink as usual Moet, confetti, candles, and roses.

We got to the hotel and checked in. On the way there she texted me and told me that she would be out all day in a meeting downtown and that she would not be back in her room until later on that evening, so I knew that I had time to set up everything the way I wanted, to surprise her.

I drove forty-five minutes to the nearest *"Gucci"* store and bought two pairs of infant baby shoes, one for a girl and one for a boy. I dropped off the sonogram picture at the *"CVS"* to have it blown up. I picked up everything I needed and headed back to the hotel. Dahlia went to her room and said that she would check on me in a few. I figured I had time to get everything done before Zayle got back from her meeting. I caught myself resting my hand on my stomach a lot and talking to the baby.

I even caught myself looking at my reflection in the mirror side ways to see if I had a bulge. I was lucky with my first two pregnancies because my stomach went right back.

It didn't look as if I would be that lucky this time, since my stomach already looked swollen as Dahlia pointed out to me when she told me that I was to kindly take off my *"Rock and Republic"* jeans since I would no longer be able to wear them.

The room was beautiful. I ordered four- dozen blue and another four dozen pink balloons. I filled the room with balloons that were shaped like pacifiers and baby bottles. It was beautiful. I even set up the bathroom with the candles and set out the *"Moet"* to chill. By this time I was starving and ready to eat. I called Dahlia and asked her if she was ready to go and get something to eat.

Although I was only eight weeks pregnant, I was already having cravings, and right now I was craving seafood. She agreed and we met in the lobby, since our rooms weren't side by side. We met up and I decide to head up the one flight to Zayle's room door and push a note under her door. The room sounded quiet so I knew she was not there.

We took the elevator downstairs to the lobby and asked a bell hop to direct us to the dining room. He told us it was right down the hall to the left of the main conference hall. We were so busy walking and talking that I had to do a double look, when I saw Zayle's sister standing to left of me in front of the conference room. She looked at me and turned extremely pale as if she were looking at a ghost.

"Hi, Nicole, what are you doing here?" I asked her with a puzzled look on my face.

She stuttered as she answered me, "Oh hi, what are you doing here?"

Ok, I noticed that she didn't answer my question, but I just continued. "I came to surprise your sister, I have some good news for her so I guess since you're here I'll tell you too".

Before I could say anything else to her the conference doors opened and out walked Tione, Zayles best friend. She walked straight into me.

Dahlia and I looked at each other, "What the fuck is really going on in here?"

Dahlia stepped in front of me and pushed open the double doors. All I heard was Dahlia yell "Oh hell no, what the fuck is this shit?"

I burst in right behind her, and could not believe my fucking eyes. There right in front of me stood Zayle and Suzanne, under an arch with a banner that read "WELCOME   TO ZAYLE AND SUZANNE'S COMMMITMENT CEREMONY"

Everyone in the conference room turned around and stared at Dahlia and I standing there looking puzzled. What hurt even more was the fact that the same people who were at my so-called engagement party was at this fucking commitment shit. Is this shit for real?

Zayle turned around and looked as if she wanted to faint. Suzanne turned around to her and asked her, "Zayle, what the fuck is this bitch doing here ruining my day?"

Before Zayle could even answer her I walked right up to her and slapped the shit out of her.

Her face turned instantly red and she looked as if she wanted to hit me back so I dared her. "I dare you Zayle. You want to hit me, go ahead. This is your fucking business meeting Zayle?"

"Nai, don't do this. Let me speak to you outside please."

"Outside? Zayle you cannot be serious, do you think I am blind? I see the sign says commitment ceremony, you're marrying this bitch?"

I knew I was crazy because the place seemed to be filled with Suzanne's family but at this point I didn't give a fuck. The judge asked them if they wanted to take a break and continue the ceremony in a few minutes.

Suzanne turned to Zayle; "I have had enough of you and this fucking bitch Zaye! Get rid of her now! Why is she stalking you?'

I got right up in her face before Zayle or Dahlia could pull me back?

"Bitch I'm stalking her? Where the fuck you think she is every fucking night Suzanne?" and then I had to flash her the ring, and oh yeah, I'm the bitch that she engaged."

She yelled right back at me, 'Well, I am the bitch she's marrying."

She got me there, she was right. I stood there embarrassed. I wanted to die. I hauled off to punch Suzanne when Dahlia grabbed my hand and yelled out "Naia the baby, don't!!!"

Zayle turned around so fast that I don't know how she didn't spark a fire. "Baby? What baby?" "Dahlia, what are you talking about?"

I swear I felt as if I was in a play because at this point everyone was perched up in their seats looking and listening to see what the hell was going on.

Some of Suzanne's family members started to curse at me and yell that I was the bitch that was trying to break up their cousin's happy home. Happy home? I had to explain to them that I was not some regular chick on the side. They didn't know who the hell they were messing with.

"Naia, let's get the fuck out of here!" She turned to Zayle and continues, "The baby will be better off without you anyway, you're a fucked up individual!"

"Dahlia, what baby are you talking about?" Then she turned to me, "Naia, are you pregnant?"

"You know what Zayle, does it really fucking matter anymore? But yes I am eight weeks pregnant with the baby that you asked me for. The baby you begged me to have. Fuck you!"

I turned to walk away and then I remembered that I had the sonogram picture in my pocket book. I turned back, and handed her the picture. "By the way congratulations!"

I couldn't even cry. In a way I wanted to bust Suzanne's ass. Even though she was a drug addict she was right. No matter what Zayle said or did in the end she was still marrying her. It didn't matter if my ring was two carrots or ten, she was committing to her.

What the fuck is wrong with me? I get played by men and women? The universe must have it out for me. Now I am pregnant for a woman, and still getting fucking played. I couldn't find the tears to cry. Dahlia just kept on hugging me and asking if I was ok. I felt numb.

I didn't know how to feel. Once again she has played me for a fool and this time it's worse, there is a baby involved. We get back to the room and Dahlia tells me that she is going to take a shower and that she will be right back. I close the door and realize that once again I am alone. Why is it that I always end up alone? What am I going to do is all that I keep asking myself. I look around the room and realize that I must be the dumbest woman in the world to be played by a woman and a man. This is crazy.

I look down at my stomach, and can't believe what I really did. I call Zayle " Hello?"

"Get your ass in my room right fucking now, room 305", and I hung up the phone. I really didn't care if she was at the alter. If she knew what I knew, she would get her ass to my room, quick fast and in a hurry. Within five minutes there was a knock on my door.

"Naia, are we really having a baby?"

"Zayle you have to be fucking kidding me. Having a baby where? You were just downstairs marrying fucking Suzanne!"

"Naia, I had to!"

"Had to what?" I walked over and chucked her in her chest.

"Why the fuck did you propose to me, Zayle? Why didn't you just leave me the hell alone? Two years Zayle. For two years, I waited on you. You come and propose to me for this? I got pregnant for this?"

"Naia, all my property was in her name. Naia, that is the only reason why I was doing this."

"Zayle, give me a fucking break. You don't have to marry someone because of property? Isn't this the same woman who fucked up your money? Who you recently found out cheated on you?"

"Naia please… How far along are you?"

"Zayle, I am eight weeks pregnant. I just found out and I came here to surprise you, but hey, the surprise is on me huh?"

She started to cry. "Naia, I love you."

"Fuck you Zayle!"

"What about the baby, Naia?"

"What about the baby? You don't worry, I'll go home, fuck some man and give it to him!"

"Anaiyah, I will fucking kill you!"

"Bitch try! Now get the fuck out of my room."

"Anaiyah, I am serious I will go to jail for you and this baby!"

"Zayle, you should have thought about that shit before you fucking married Suzanne.'

"Anaiyah, you stopped it before any papers got signed."

"I really don't give a fuck, get out of my room and go back to your so called business meeting."

I grabbed the *"Gucci"* bag with the baby shoes in it and threw it at her. "You will need this to remember us by and by the way, I'll have my lawyer draw up the papers to undo the shit you made me sign"

"NAIA STOP BEING IRRATIONAL !"

"IRRATIONAL ZAYLE! YOU CANNOT BE SERIOUS!"

I couldn't see. The rage was blinding me and all I wanted was to hurt her right now. How could she? She walked over to me and started to kiss me just as if just a few seconds ago I wasn't even screaming at her at the top of my lungs and about to literally wrap my hands around her throat to choke the life out of her. The funny thing is I am kissing her back. I am actually enjoying it. What the hell is going on with me? Could it be the hormones?   I am kissing her back as if it's the last time. As a matter of fact this will be our last time.

"Make love to me Zayle, that's all I want right now. You don't want to spend your life with me at least I know the sex is good. You want that right, so go ahead take it."

I step back from her and start to undress. Recklessly throwing my clothes around the hotel room. Not an ounce of seductiveness in me. I didn't care. This was going to be the last time we slept together so I was going to make it good. Especially now since I am pregnant,

I can't sleep with anyone else. So why not shit. This is ridiculous. I walk over to her and press against her, pushing her into the desk. She gestured as if to say stop, but I silenced her with a kiss. She tries to ease me off of her.

"What's the matter Zayle? You fucked Suzanne already so now you can't sleep with me, what the fuck you're being faithful now, is that it?"

"Fuck her? Naia I'm not in love with her, why would I fuck her?"

"Not in love with her? That's funny and surprising since you were just downstairs in the conference room committing to her. You're funny!"

"No, Naia! I'm not going to do that and you know that you really don't want to."

"Zayle, please all I want right now is for you to make love to me please. Zayle, just fuck me and go your way, go be with your bitch!"

I start to kiss her again feverishly almost with hate. This is so confusing, I am feeling hate for her, but it's so passionate that it's turning me on. Is this because the saying is true that there is a thin line between love and hate? I know that's the case and I do both with a great deal of passion. I love with passion and I hate with passion. Both can and always get me in trouble.

I continue to kiss her disregarding the fact that she is steadfastly trying to push me off of her trying her best not to kiss me; except she taught me the art of seduction. She used it on me. Now it was my turn to use it on her.

"Look me in my eyes Zayle, and tell me right now that you don't want me. If you can do that, I'll stop right now."

She couldn't say a word. She grasped my face and started to kiss me back, GOTCHA. We made love just like that, like nothing was wrong. Sweat dripping off of our bodies only to be interrupted five minutes into it by her phone vibrating on the desk.

She actually motioned as if she were really going to answer it. She must be out of her fucking mind.   I grab her and pull her on top of me..

"Eat me Zayle, now."

She didn't hesitate and she slid down to the perfect position. I raised up my legs, opening my legs to allow her to do what she always did with such passion, what led me to believe that she loved me and that I was the only woman for her. For sixty minutes, I felt that my world was her world. That everything was ok and she was mine, all mine. Her tongue action always made me forget what the hell I was mad at, but not this time. This was the "finale". After I came the fifth time in her mouth that was it, I made sure to tire her ass out.

"Now fuck that go kiss your bitch, I'm done."

I slammed the door in her face, I could see that she was crying, but who gave a fuck, not me.

Now I am feeling nauseous, I grab my belly and tell my baby that it will all be ok. I have to head back to Brooklyn and call my lawyer to undo the joint custody papers between Zayle and myself. The only good thing was that she also put in the papers that she would pay child support and health insurance for the baby, even if we didn't reside under the same roof or if we didn't have domestication papers. At this point I am feeling so depressed.

What am I going to do? I open the mini bar. Maybe I need a drink, I'm only weeks pregnabt it won't hurt the baby. I call my mom to check on the kids, they're at a birthday party and they could barely hear me but I yell to them that I love them, and told them to call me later.

I open a bottle of vodka. I look in my handbag and I have a bottle of painkillers. Maybe I should end it all. Why bring an innocent baby into all this drama. My cell phone is going off. One behind the other Zayle and her sister are calling me. What the hell are they calling me for now? I have nothing to say. The tears are falling now and I can't stop them. I am tired of crying, tired of being hurt, tired of feeling alone, and tired of feeling as if I am not good enough.

I fell in love with my best friend, didn't care that she was a woman, and here we go again. She is playing me worse than any man has ever played me. As long as I have been alive a man never got me pregnant and played me. Here my dumb ass is allowing a woman to do this, I must be nuts. A few months ago someone sexually violated me and now someone whom I love is betraying me. I can't take it anymore. My children are with my mother; they will be taken care of.

I pour out the glass of vodka into a glass and open the bottle of pills. My baby and I don't need this, maybe we will be at peace if I just end it all.

Chapter 19

I woke up with such an intense headache I thought my head was about to split open. The first thing I did was throw up. My God when will the morning sickness end? Thank God Dahlia drove all the way back. Between my crying and throwing up, I would have never made it home. I have so many decisions to make right now. First and foremost, I need to decide if I am going to keep my baby. Every time I look at the picture, I realize how beautiful the baby is. Wow I still cannot believe that it happened so quickly. There was a knock at my door. My God, I can't even throw up in peace.

"Who is it?"

"Me, Ian."

"Hi baby." I opened the door and gave him a hug.

"Naia, first thing first congratulations, we did it huh?", he bent down and kissed my stomach. "Mom called me and told me what happened in D.C. Naia I had no clue."

"Ian, it's ok. I just have to think about my children now, especially this baby."

I walk over and get the sonogram picture out of my pocket book.

"Have you ever seen anything so beautiful? She looks like a sea horse, but still."

We both started to laugh out loud.

"How do you know it is a she? Naia am I missing something?" he said this as he was turning the poor sonogram picture up, down, and every which way.

"No. I'm just eight weeks, but until I know for sure, I guess it's a she," I said as I snatched my picture.

His visit was short and sweet and I was ever so happy. Now I have to decide, if I am going to call Darren over, sleep with him and give him the baby. Problem is I haven't slept with him in what a year and a half now. Getting him to sleep with me won't be a problem; it's the age of the pregnancy.

Shit, I didn't change my locks, so I can't have him come over here. Knowing Zayle, her ass may just pop up at anytime. I really don't want to use him, but I don't know have any other male friends right now. Maybe I will just ask Ian to participate in the baby's life with me.

I decide I am tired of thinking. I want to go out and party before my ass can't go anymore.

"Dahlia, do you feel like going out with me to a gay club tonight?"

"Nai, I just want you to stop crying. It's not good for you or the baby. I'll be there at 12 ok."

"Cool"

It was already 11:00 p.m. and I slept the entire day away. I loved living in New York, the only town you can find a club to party in on a Sunday night. I throw on a simple pair of jeans and a black shirt.

I had to leave the button open, but hey the shirt covered it. I'm feeling so sick to my stomach that I decide to go into my kitchen and drink a glass of ginger ale to settle it. Suddenly there is a knock on my door. It was Dahlia ready to go.

On the drive there she is bombarding me with all these different baby names. She drove me mad, but I love her, and right now she is my support system. So I will deal with her madness for now. She even told me about her plans to place a crib in her room. That was funny since the girl could sleep through a hurricane. Her roof could be ripped completely off and she wouldn't know shit until it was over.

We finally join the line and it is long as hell, but Dahlia worked her magic and got us right in.

"Nai, do me a favor, throw up AWAY from me if you have to, thank you".

We both laughed, but in my head I was trying to remind myself, since I seemed to have no control over when or where I threw up. In less than two hours I was ready to leave. My feet hurt and I was tired. Thank God Dahlia was ready also, so we got ourselves together and headed for the door. As soon as we stepped out of the club, all I could feel was someone grab my hand and spin me around.

"What the hell are you doing in a club and you're pregnant?"

"Excuse me, Zayle! Don't ask me any questions, go and ask your fucking bitch at home!"

"Anaiyah, for God's sake. Please don't make lose my fucking temper with you. Take your ass home, with my baby."

"Your baby?"

Poor Dahlia is standing in between us and trying to tell us that we were causing a scene. Of course both of us couldn't care less who the hell was watching. The funny thing was that we never argued before or cursed at each other. We made a promise to never curse at each other or argue in public but after this weekend all bets are off.

"NAIA GO HOME!"

"You know what Zayle, I was already heading home. Not because of you, but because I am tired. But guess what I won't be alone."

As soon as those words came out of my mouth, I hurried and walked away because I knew from the look in her eyes, she was about to lose it. Good I got to her, and that was my intention.

I had to hear Dee lecture me all the way home about losing my temper, and that getting angry like that was no good for the baby. As soon as she dropped me off, I hopped into my bed, called the kids, spoke with them for a few minutes and went to sleep.

The prayer I prayed that night I believe had to be the most honest prayer I have ever prayed.

"Dear God,

It's me Naia, please God, I don't know what to do, but I leave it all up to you."

Chapter 20

onths have passed and I am now sixteen weeks pregnant. I haven't seen Zayle in two months. I even changed my home number, and of course she got it as soon as I changed it. Being a lawyer and having all of my information especially my social security number, made it as easy as typing my name into the computer, and all of my information was on a computer screen.

What made it easier also was the simple fact that she knew I could not change my cell phone number because of the practice. They finally made me an offer to become a senior partner, which would finally up my salary to at least ten thousand a week. On the day that the partners made me an offer, I received four dozen beautiful red roses at the office. The card simply said, "From me to u, I love u"; but I knew it was from Zayle because that use to be our secret code, for everything, 'From me to u."

How she found out I really couldn't tell you but the girl was good. I ignored every single phone call and text message that she sent. She even started to deposit money in my bank account four hundred dollars a week. I knew it was her because every single week I would have an extra four hundred dollars in my account. The problem was I missed her. I was never able to sleep with Darren, I couldn't do it; it just wasn't me. My friends at work were all excited about the baby, except they all wanted to meet the father, and how could I explain to them that there was no father, and that my lover was with another woman.

I really felt alone. Even the kids couldn't understand. Ok mommy is pregnant, but we never see her with a man, only "Auntie Zayle".

My parents, well they were happy, because they figured at least we have confirmation, that she is not gay. My mom especially quickly called all her girlfriends to spread the news, "Oh, Anaiyah is having a baby!" She even made the kids stay there now with her on a full time basis, since I have been so sick and with my schedule at work. Ian and their mom, checked on me frequently making meals for me everyday. Everyone was happy, except me. I missed her, I really did. But I didn't know what to do.

Today was my first official sonogram appt to find out the baby's sex, and I am going alone. No one to hold my hand. No one to get excited with me. Dahlia offered to go with me but I told her that it was ok. I knew that she had a few patients scheduled. She has done so much for me already. I couldn't let her do that.

My stomach had swollen so fast that I looked as if I was already six months pregnant. I threw on a sweat suit, since that was the only thing besides my scrubs that I was comfortable in, threw on my *"Hogan"* sneakers and headed to the doctors office.

On my way there; I started to cry. I can't believe that I am doing this all alone again. They said the third time's a charm, so where is my charm?

All the women in the doctor's office were usually there with their husbands and I was always there by myself or with Dahlia. Zayle always wanted to come to the doctor's appointments but I couldn't bear to see her right now.

168

I didn't want to get use to her being around me anymore and I had someone more important to think about right now. Dahlia kept her up to date on my doctor's appointments even though I didn't agree with it, but she had a point. I didn't do this alone; she asked me to have this baby. If she were a man it wouldn't have been any different.

She still has an obligation to me; and this child. I arrived to the appointment a few minutes late, I had a sudden urge for a banana split. Now this is ridiculous, it is freezing outside, and I want a banana split. I walked into the office finishing up my ice cream, and the secretary started to laugh at me. I had to let her know that this baby had completely taken me over.

I entered the examination room and hopped up on the table. I looked at my stomach, "Well sweetheart today mommy finds out if you are a girl or a boy. Either way I will be happy."
Dr. MacIntire came into the room. He wanted to do the sonogram himself, instead of the technician.

"Naia, do you understand how luck you are. You got pregnant on the first try, and the way you did it... just please don't tell my patients I'll lose business."

I laughed, "No, I would never do that. Yeah I guess I am lucky huh?"

He placed the Doppler on my stomach and I heard "Swish, swish, swish, swish... "

"Oh my God! That is beautiful." The sound of my baby's heartbeat was music to my ears.

I asked him to use the internal video, so that my children could hear and see their brother's or sister's heart beat and see the miracle of life. He then turned on the machine and there my baby was.

"There's the head, the feet, the hands, ten fingers…ten toes" In the middle of him describing my baby, his nurse knocks on the door.

"Dr. MacIntire and Dr. Williams, I am sorry to interrupt you, but there is someone here demanding to be let into the room."

Before she said another word, I knew exactly who it was, no one but Zayle. She stepped in front of the nurse.

"Dr. MacIntire, I'm sorry, but please I need to speak to Naia."

He excused himself and said he'd be right back.

"Naia please, I understand that you hate me, but this is our baby. Please just let me be a part of it all, please, I know I fucked up", I could barely understand her because she was crying so hard. My first reaction was to throw her ass straight out of there but this was a special day, and I wanted to share it with someone so why not her.

She placed her head on my stomach and cried. "Babe, you are getting the gel all over your face."

"Nai, I really don't care, please just let me stay."

Jim entered back into the room. He knew the story between us, so there was no need to explain anything to him. Thank God.

He started over so that she could hear the baby's heart beat. He showed us the head the toes, all the limbs were there. We both started to smile and laugh. We actually saw the baby do a flip.

"Do you guys want to know the sex?"

She nodded yes, and I replied, "Yes"

Except the baby's legs were closed.

Zayle placed her lips to my stomach and whispered "My sweet baby, please let us know what you are.'

And just like that as if he actually understood what she asked of him and our son opened his legs.

.

"You guys have a boy," as he showed us his penis.

"Oh my God Naia, we have a son!" she started to yell and pump her fists in the air as if she won the lottery. I have known this woman for more than ten years, and I've never seen her this way before, ever.

I then began to cry uncontrollably. I have a son, wow! I have two daughters, and now a son. I asked Jim if we could have a few minutes alone, I just wanted to stare at him for a while. He left the room, and I took the Doppler and gave it to her.

"Baby, run this slowly over my belly please. I can't believe we have a son."

As I handed her the wand, she saw that I still had my engagement ring on. "Baby, you're still wearing my ring?"

"Yes, I know I am a fool, but that is all I have left of you besides my son now."

"Naia, stop that please. I want to be a part of you and my son's life. Please let me?"

"Zayle, you have hurt me in a way that I can never even begin to explain. You betrayed me. I gave you all of me, and trusted you, and you just didn't give a fuck." I told her that I really didn't want to discuss anything like that right now.

"Zaye, print out a few pictures if you want, since this will be the last time that you see me or him."

We both started to cry and I just turned my head the other way. I couldn't afford to let her break me down now. I have a few more months to go, and I mentally prepared myself to deal with it. I can't turn back now. She printed out her pictures, helped me get dressed and we walked out the office together. She asked me if she could come by the house tomorrow to pick up the truck and have it winterized. I told her no that I would take care of it myself.

Hopped in my truck, and went home. I could see her just standing there through my rear view mirror; but why should I forgive her now? She did this to me. I didn't do anything to her. She proposed to me and turned around and committed to someone else. Her being a woman doesn't make it any different. Ok yes it is a lot different because it is not the same thing as a man and woman.

But it is just as serious.

172

Chapter 21

I walk in my house, and a sea of loneliness overtakes my body. My house is so quiet that I can literally hear the steam coming up through the pipes. It is funny how you can know a thousand people or more and yet still feel lonely. I am alone. I am feeling very unloved at this moment, and I don't know how to break this feeling that has suddenly come over me. It doesn't help that my raging hormones have me an emotional wreck.

I kick off my sneakers and turn on the television. I am hungry but my feet hurt and I am really too tired to get myself something to eat. These are the moments that I stop and wonder, why have I always tried to be such a great woman to anyone that I was in a relationship with. I know why I did it, I always hoped that the person I was with would reflect the way I treated them and treat me the exact same way.

Sadly that was never the case. It always seemed as if my kindness and love would get taken for a sign of weakness. Zayle would treat me the exact same way I treated her but then in an instant, things could and would go sour.

It's almost Christmas and I haven't bought one gift much less thought of whom I would be buying gifts for. The baby was due in May and I haven't bought a thing for him either. See, that is why I missed Zayle. She was always so organized. All these things would have been taken care of already. We actually complimented each other in that way. I would come up with the plans and she would execute them.

I was the procrastinator and she was the go-getter. If she could only learn to appreciate me.

My son starts to move. It startled me, to the point that I jumped. I forgot how funny it felt to feel a baby move inside of you. Yes everyone is right when they say it feels like gas, but it also tickles. I took out my cell phone, took off my shirt and took a picture of my belly for Zayle. I contemplated on whether or not to send it for at least a half hour.

Dahlia called me several times and I just didn't feel like speaking. What was I going to say? The same thing that I have been saying for several months now over and over? Nothing has changed.

In the midst of my contemplating my life, there is a knock at my door. I didn't feel like having company, so I ignored it. I figured the person would get the hint and leave.

"Who is it?

"It's me Nina."

"Oh shit." I flung open the door, "Girl what are you doing here? How are you?"

"I'm fine, I flew in today and just took a chance that you might be home."

We gave each other a big hug and stepped back to look at each other.

"Naia, is that a belly I see?" ,she said while rubbing my belly.

"YES!"

174

She takes my two hands and holds them up in front of her to get a good look at my stomach, and sees my ring,

"Oh my God, where is Darren? Let me congratulate him!"

"Well, how can I say this, there's no way to say it than to just say it, so here goes. The baby is Zayles."

"Huh, you mean Zayle from college, you're carrying her baby?"

"No, I fell in love with her, got inseminated by her brother, and we are having a baby."

She must have felt as if she was in the twilight zone, I could see on her face that she was trying to figure it all out. Figure out how the hell I was pregnant with Zayles baby. Wasn't I straight, and always denying that something was going on between Zayle and I.

"Oh my God I am happy for you! See we always use to tease you guys about being together."

I had to explain to her that no, we really were not together in school. That this all happened long after graduation. I didn't bother to play myself and let her know that she also played me. We chatted for about an hour and then she left.

I decided to call it an early night and headed for the shower. Every time my hands came across my baby, I would start to wonder if I made the right decisions in my life. I came out and settled for bed.

My phone rang with an unknown call, which usually was the answering service for the office, but I am not on call tonight, so why would they call me.

"Hello, Dr. Williams, here."

"LISTEN BITCH! IF YOU THINK ZAYLE WILL HAVE ANYTHING TO DO WITH YOUR FUCKING BABY YOU HAVE ANOTHER THING COMING!!"

Ok this bitch must have lost her mind, calling my house.

"Suzanne listen to me, do not under any circumstance let my belly fool you. I will kick your ass ok, and don't you ever call this fucking number again!"

I hung up the phone. That did not stop her, she must have called my phone a thousand times yelling and screaming into my answering machine. I refused to answer her. I got out of my bed, and got dressed. I couldn't even find my sweat suit top, and my belly was sticking out from under my undershirt, but I didn't give a fuck. I headed straight over to Zayle's house.

I didn't call her, and I didn't call Dahlia. I didn't want anyone stopping me from going over there. For two years, I never fucked with her, even though she knew about me, I stayed out of her way, but she was not about to harass my baby and me.

I got to the house, walked right up and stuck my finger on the bell. Zayle came to the door; looking as confused as a deer in headlights.

"I didn't come here for you! Where the fuck is your bitch, tell her to come to the door!"

"Naia, what the hell is going on? What you want to see Suzanne for?"

"Zayle your bitch has been calling my house all night cursing about me and the baby."

At the same moment Suzanne came running up behind Zayle.

"Let me at your bitch Zayle! You and her think you gonna bring this baby in this fucking world, fuck the both of you!'

Zayle slapped her dead in her mouth. I was so shocked, that I didn't even react.

"Sue, you will not speak about my child like that, we had this discussion already. You can get the fuck out, but you won't disrespect my child!"

She then turned to me grabbed me by my arm and started yelling at me.

"And you, you know better! What the fuck are you doing out of your house at this time of night in the cold, with your belly all out?"

I yanked my arm away from her so violently I thought I pulled it out of the socket.

"Zayle leave me the hell alone, and control your bitch!"

Just as I turned to walk away Sue, came charging at me, with her leg raised as if she were gonna kick me in my stomach. Luckily I had a can of mace in my hand that I had bought off of the streets in *"China Town"*, and just as she got around Zayle, I maced her. She fell flat on the ground screaming.

"You bitch! I'm gonna fuck you up, and kick that baby out of you!"

I went to kick her as she lay on the ground screaming but Zayle grabbed me and lifted me up.

She placed me in my car, and slammed the door shut. Jumped in the driver's side and started the car.

"Didn't I tell you to return my car key?"

"Nai, I love you, now shut up, I'm taking you home."

I wanted to argue with her but now my head was pounding. She must have realized that something was wrong with me, because she leaned over and adjusted my seat for me to lean back further. We pulled up into my driveway and went into my house.

"Naia, I am not even gonna get at you for this shit tonight because you know better, and that's our baby, that you are jeopardizing."

"Get at me? Zayle are you fucking kidding me? This bitch called me? I let you go I don't even call you."

"Anaiyah, what don't you understand, I love you! Not her."

"Zayle what don't you understand? You married her not me, and left me pregnant, you did some shit a nigga on the street would do."

I knew I hit a nerve with that. She stopped dead in her tracks, and fell to her knees.

She held on to my waist and rested her head on my belly, and just cried.

"Naia, I want to hear his heart beat please."

She placed her lips to my belly and started to speak to him.

"Son, I am so sorry that I hurt your mommy like this, but I swear to you that I love her, and I love you. I messed up, but I will make it up to you both."

After all of this excitement, I was ready to go to my bed. I grabbed her hands and raised her to her feet. I knew I should have told her to leave, but I didn't want to be alone.

I led her to my bed, it felt weird having her in my bed again. I had gotten use to sleeping alone. She seemed hesitant but didn't resist. I changed my clothes, and handed her boxers and a wife beater. She looked surprised that I still had her clothes there. She went to take a shower, and I just climbed into bed.

The next thing I knew she was in the bed curled up behind me with her hand resting on my stomach. I felt funny. I didn't feel as if I was still attractive to her. She kept trying to turn me over to look at me, but I resisted telling her that I felt more comfortable laying on my side. She starts to rub my belly.

At least for tonight, I wasn't alone.

Chapter 22

A nyone who has ever had a baby can tell you that the months fly by so quickly. I am now 38 weeks pregnant and I look as if I am about to burst at the seams at any given moment. I haven't been at work in two months because the doctor put me on maternity leave. I have Partial Placenta Previa and he couldn't risk me going into labor at all. It would be too dangerous for the baby and for me due to the fact that if I went into labor the placenta would come out before the baby and then the baby would not be able to breathe.

Zayle has been coming around but I am still playing hard to get. I am scared and it's getting harder to do because I am getting hornier by the hours. I haven't made love or had sex since she and I last slept together and that was about eight months ago. Whenever she stays over now it is as if she is scared to touch me.

I spent most of my days sitting in court watching her trial her cases. She amazed me. The girl was good at what she does, she was born to debate. I loved to watch her argue her cases. She was on a roll and I am so proud of her. But today I am not going to sit in this court all day. I want seafood, and this boy is hungry. He was now doing flips and turns, and my belly had now become an amusement show.

Dahlia and Zayle's new past time was to sit and watch my belly do flips. The kids would sit there and try to figure out where exactly his foot was in my stomach and tickle him. There my baby was, arguing her case and commanding the attention of the entire courtroom.

I couldn't let her know exactly how proud I was of her, because I am not giving in. She insisted that I stayed in her sight every single minute, especially since the c-section was scheduled for next week Thursday. I couldn't even go to the store without her.

Suzanne was still there, but she knew better than to mess with me. I decided that after I had the baby I would give Zaye an ultimatum, either me and the baby or Suzanne, but somebody had to go. There was not room for all of us. Whatever she did, she got Suzanne in check because since that night she didn't fuck with me. The only person that was harassing me was Darren, and Zayle got one of her colleagues, to slap him with a restraining order. I was so tired of his harassment. Every night this man would call my house and call me a lesbian, among other things. He would yell at me on my phone saying me and my dyke girlfriend can go to hell. The only problem was that he still had to see the children. So I made sure that he would pick them up at my mom's house.

I started looking for my new house and I found the perfect one. I am scheduled to move in after the baby is born. Zayle chose and paid for all of his furniture, but I told her not to have it delivered, until I gave birth.

Ok now I am starving. As soon as the judge called for a recess, summoned her over, "Baby, I am hungry! I am going to call Dahlia so she can come with me to get some seafood ok?"

"Ok baby call her, and I will meet you guys at the restaurant ok?"

I kept calling Dahlia but I kept going to her voicemail.

"Baby, she must be with a patient, I am not getting an answer."

At that same moment the judge entered the court and ordered a continuance for the next day. I was never so happy; this boy was about to make sure that I ate.

"Baby, look at my stomach, he is hungry." We both had to laugh because my stomach looked like a one sided basketball. He had moved all the way over to one side, and decided to stretch out. She knew that I was now using him as my way of getting spoiled.

She started to laugh, "Baby, you know by next week you won't have any more excuses to get spoiled, right?"

I held her face close to mine, "No your wrong, for the rest of your life I will have an excuse for you to spoil me,... our son!"

With that I leaned in and started to kiss her. I knew at that moment I was caught. Again! We hadn't kissed in so long that I forgot how sweet her kisses felt, and how passionate they were. I instantly got wet.

"Baby fuck the food, please take me home and make love to me?"

"Are you sure? Naia are you sure, you want me?"
"Positive!"

We drove all the way home in silence just holding hands. It felt strange as if this was our first time. It had been so long with everything that was going on in our lives and between us. I was actually nervous. Except she didn't drive to my house, she drove to her house.

"What about Suzanne?" She didn't answer me. She just started to kiss me passionately, taking off my clothes.

Once she got to my naked belly, she just stared and then started to kiss me over and over. "Babe, thank you, thank you, so much, you are so strong and brave thank you!" She didn't allow me to answer her, she just kept kissing me. I felt nervous, not knowing where Suzanne was, but I trusted her that she wouldn't put the baby or myself in harms way, so I just relaxed. This was not the first time that we made love in her house.

It's just that this time I feel vulnerable. I guess because I know that my belly is so big that if anything were to go down with Suzanne and I, I wouldn't be able to defend myself. Sure Zaye would defend me, but hey I am a fighter by nature.

She asked me to take a seat on the chair and just wait for her. She got her digital camera and asked me to just pose for her. I felt a little awkward but at the same time I felt sexy. I had new life inside of me. I turned and posed, as if I were on *"America's Next Top Model"*. She put the camera down and walked over to me. She started to kiss me from head to toe.

Oh My God, I thought I was going to lose my mind. I took her hands and placed them on my breasts, they were so swollen and tender, but I was dying for her to touch them. Well I really wanted her to suck them but she kept saying that she felt funny.

"Baby, how can you feel funny? What do you mean?"
She never answered me, she just went back down, and slowly parted my legs. I almost jumped out of my seat. It was hard for me to maneuver my body with my belly in front of me. And then she stopped.

"Baby, I can't! I feel as if I'm violating my son."

"Zayle, I need sex ok. I am horny I haven't done anything since you months ago."

"You better had not!"

"Shut up then and give me some dick," I said to her.

"Are you serious? Nah babe, you can't."

"Zayle, strap on and give me some dick, I am very serious."

"Anaiyah, are you sure?"

I guess she was referring to the fact that since the incident with Warren I never asked for sex with a dildo, and then I got pregnant so quickly afterwards, which was without "dick", but I felt for it now, and that is what mattered. She went in the bathroom and strapped on. For some reason after all these years, she still wouldn't strap on in front of me, which was ridiculous to me, but hey that was her. She strapped on and came out.

"Ok, babe lay on your back please? That is the only way I think I will feel comfortable with my belly."

She lay back on the bed, and helped me straddle over her and work my way over her. I took my hands and guided the dick to my pussy. My face grimaced in pain because there was no way that this 12inch dick was just going to glide in, after all this time.

I eased my way on to it. "Oh shit babe!"

"Are you ok? Baby, let's stop."

Is she kidding me this was feeling so fucking good, painful, yet good. I did not want to stop at all. I moved and worked my way on it as if there was no tomorrow.

"Nai, please be careful, your pregnant."

I didn't even stop to answer, I couldn't I was about to come. Within minutes I came. All I could do was scream. There was nothing else for me to say or do. She started to laugh at me.

I felt embarrassed because she started to laugh at me.

"Look at you, you little freak! Nine months pregnant and still want to fuck."

I started laughing too but she was right though. Sex was one thing we always had in common and it was always great. By the time I was ready to go home morning came. I kissed her good bye and went home. I didn't want to wake her, since I knew she would have to be in court all day today.

Things are looking up for us now, I am so happy. Everything is going well. I'm scared to get happy though, because as the old saying goes, "After the calm comes the storm".

Chapter 23

T he wetness of the sheets woke me out of my sleep quickly. "Please don't tell me that my bladder has finally failed me." I jumped out of my sleep, and ran to the bathroom, well waddled is more of what I did. I sat on the toilet and the stream just kept on running until I noticed that it wouldn't stop. I got up changed my clothes and sheets; and by the time I walked back to get in the bed, I was soaking again.

"OH SHIT DID MY WATER BREAK?"

I call Zayle quickly and no answer as usual. I left her a message, "Please, please call me, I think my water broke."

I call Dahlia, "Hey Dee, please come over, I think my water broke."

"Naia, are you serious? I am coming over right now"

I hung up and went to take a shower, I wanted to be clean before the doctors started to poke and prod me. I called my mother to let her know that I was in labor, and that I would let her know when I was on my way to the hospital. While I was in the shower, Dahlia used her key to come in to the house. If there ever was a time that I was happy to see her, today was the day. She came in and helped me out of the shower, and that is when the first contraction hit me. "Oh shit, D! Girl I just had a contraction."

"Naia come and lay down, where is Zayle, did you call her?"

"I called her and left her a voice mail and texted her, she still hasn't called me back."

I told her that I needed to get some sleep and rest up, for the labor part. I knew that was going to kick my ass. Then I called my Doctor and told him to book the O.R. for later that evening, that my water had broken, but since I was a Doctor also, he gave me a little leeway to monitor myself. At this point they were coming once every hour.

I asked Dahlia to continue to call Zayle for me and tell her to come straight over to the house that I was in labor. The pain woke me out of my sleep, in less than an hour. I asked Dahlia to take me to the hospital. We still hadn't heard from Zayle, but the contractions were getting worse and I couldn't afford to go in to full active labor. On the way to the hospital, Darren called me, I answered him.

"Darren, please go get the kids from mom for me."

"Naia, what's wrong? Are you crying?"

I tried to contain the pain in my voice but this shit was kicking my ass. Poor Dahlia was a wreck; she's driving and panicking at the same time. I placed the cell on speaker and it was sheer pain to even speak. Dahlia screams into the phone, "Darren, I'm taking Nai to the hospital, she's in labor!"

"I'll meet you there!"

"Dahlia, do you think it is wise for Darren to meet us at the hospital? Call Zayle again please!"

"Anaiyah, I am not calling Zayle's ass again! She knows you're about to have the baby! If she gave a fuck she would have called you!"

What could I say, there was nothing that I could say to even attempt to make her look good or to make myself feel any better. The pain was unbearable. As soon as we entered the emergency room they whisked me away. They could not afford to let me go into active labor and it seemed as if this boy was not going to wait. They shaved me up as quick as they could, and the anesthesiologist entered the room. "I want to be awake to welcome my son into the world," I exclaimed.

He broke a tongue depressor and scraped my shoulder and then scraped my belly to see if I could feel pain. I was so terrified he had to ask me at least three times if I was feeling pain or just the sensation of the wood scraping against my skin.

The doctor finally walked in, "Do you want anyone in the room with you?"

"Yes, please allow Dahlia in the operating room, she deserves to see her next godchild enter the world."

They quickly helped her scrub and enter the room. Darren was standing by the O.R. glass and even though we weren't on good terms, it was good to see a familiar face standing outside the glass. It felt even better to have my best friend right beside me.

How could Zayle ever explain missing the birth of our son to me? To him? To anyone? There was no way, no explanation, unless her ass was laid up under a damn truck somewhere.

Within seconds I felt them tugging at the skin. It felt so weird to actually feel hands pulling and hear the skin and old scars from my two previous C-sections popping, but not feeling the pain. This is the moment when every mom decides never again, but luckily for mankind, God or a higher power mysteriously erases the memory of the pain afterwards, or women would never have children again due to the pain.

Then the worst thing happened, I knew he was out, I could see him, but I heard no cry. Any parent will tell you that this is the worse sound you can ever hear at the time of your child's birth...silence. I start to try and raise up off the table.

"WHATS WRONG WHY ISNT HE CRYING?"

Dahlia is holding my hand, as I start to panic and scream. I can't hear the nurse telling me to calm down, that my blood pressure was going sky high.

"BITCH PLEASE FUCK MY BLOOD PRESSURE!! WHY ISN'T HE CRYING?"

Then he cried.

I cannot even begin to explain the sense of relief that came over my body on that table. He weighed in at nine pounds even and 22 ½ inches. The biggest baby I had to date. My oldest girl came in at 6 pounds 19 inches and my baby girl came in at 7 pounds 20 inches.

They explained to me that the cord was wrapped around his neck so he was going into distress. Thank God we got there when we did. The last thing I remember is seeing them wheel him out in the bassinet and Dahlia walking out behind it crying.

That was it… lights out.

Chapter 24

*T*he pain was so extreme that my eyes shot open like a deer in head lights. Wow! You would think after two previous cesarean sections I would have remembered what the pain felt like, but as I said before I think God programmed women to forget what the pain feels like. I immediately pressed the button on the side of the bed to get a little pain relief.

The nurse walked in and informed me that I must get out of the bed this morning. Although I am a doctor all my years of medical training flew out of the window, I looked at her as if she was crazy. Although I knew I had to, I really didn't feel like even moving.

I asked her to remove my catheter and sat up in the bed. I was all alone again and ready to see my son. I buzzed the nurse and asked her to bring him to me. She came in, checked my ID tag and went into the nursery to get him for me.

As she approached me with him in her arms, all I could see was a jet black head of hair poking out from under a blanket, and his little arms were flailing and he was whimpering, almost as if he was about to cry. A rush of emotions came over me. Here I am with a new son, no father, no partner, no lover, no man. NO ONE.

I still haven't heard from Zayle and I don't even know if she knows that he was born. I take him into my arms, and tell the nurse thank you. I can't help but to smile.

He looks like his sisters when they were born. I had to laugh because he was so light skin he almost looked like a Caucasian baby.

He opened up his eyes and looked at me. "Hi Sivan, I am your mommy."

I burst into tears. There is no daddy, no one else. Just me, MOMMY…

The nurses' aid enters the room with the birth certificate for me to sign. It was now time for me to officially name him. I contemplated but I knew one thing was for certain, his first name was definitely Sivan. I signed the paper... Sivan Zayle Williams. That's it.

The line for father, I left blank. Ian gave me the option to include him on it if I wanted to, but then I thought about it. Why do that? Then when I need to travel I will have to find him. Nah I'd rather just leave it blank. I'll tell Sivan, when I'm ready. He falls asleep and I buzz the nurse and ask her to return him to the nursery for me.

I call my mom, "Hey Mom…"

"Hey honey how are you feeling? How's my new grandbaby?"

"I'm in pain Mom. I forgot how much it hurts, but somehow when I see him it subsides. He's absolutely beautiful and has a full head of jet black hair."

"I can't wait to see him. The girls want to see him also."

"Good, can you bring them down this evening? I miss them too."

"Sure. Anaiyah I hope I can finally meet the baby's father when I'm there." I never explained to her the situation.

I didn't think I should have to...I am a grown ass woman. Plus I didn't need the extra stress and questions about if I am gay, if I am with a woman and all these other bullshit questions.

And still no Zayle. Our son is twenty – fours old and I don't even think that she knows that he is here.

I refuse to call her... I've already called her several times.

Chapter 25

Being in the house with a new baby felt so weird! I took off three months from work and hired a car service to take the kids to and from school for me. He dropped them at my mom's house for me and then she would bring them over around 8pm.

This was our first day home and I was trying to adjust. Zayle keeps calling my phone and I refuse to answer her. Between her and Darren I didn't know who left more messages on my phone.

Darren was calling because he wanted to see Sivan. "What the hell for," was all I kept asking him. "Take care of the two we have, don't worry about my son." I screamed at him.

I finally got Sivan to settle down. He was being a little cranky because he obviously needed some sleep and I decided to lie down and get some rest myself. We got home late the night before and he had me up all night feeding every two hours. The girls refused to go to sleep; all they wanted to do was help me. Finally I had to insist that they went to bed.

My door bell starts to ring, "DAMN, I'M COMING!" Who could it be at this hour waking me out of my sleep?

Whoever it is had to be crazy, didn't they know I just had a baby?

I scurry to the door, whispering, "Who is it?"

A low voice says, "It's me…"

My body froze because I knew exactly who it was……ZAYLE.

It was as if she sensed the hesitation in my voice.

"Nai, please open the door."

I thought for a minute. What should I do?   She leaned against the door. "Please Nai. Please let me see our son…"

I opened the door and let her in. She reached out to hug me. Is she crazy? She missed the birth of a baby that we planned together. How could I forgive her? I can't let this go. She walked into my room and headed straight for his bassinet. She leaned in and took him out.

After looking into his eyes for a few minutes she started to cry. She cried so hard that she started to tremble while holding him. I tried not to be affected but any time she broke down I would break down. I started to cry, but I couldn't let her know that I felt her pain. How could I when she caused me pain too?

I didn't say a word to her and she knew me well enough to know not to even attempt to talk to me right now. I took the opportunity to go take a shower and freshen up. It took me a while because I felt filthy. I washed my hair and scoured my skin. I had to be careful of my c-section because it wasn't completely healed but man did it feel good, I felt like I washed off ten pounds.

I came out and Zayle practically rearranged my room. The girl was a neat freak. She rearranged all of his stuff, even switching the bassinet to the other side of the bed. I didn't even say anything to her.

She had fallen asleep with him on her chest. So I took the opportunity to get some sleep myself. I went into the girl's room, and covered myself from head to toe and fell fast asleep. I had slept straight through the next day. When I looked at the clock before I fell asleep it was 1am, it was now 11pm. The girls had came home and she had given them their baths, fed them, and had them sleeping in the pull out couch camp style. They were all but too happy; this was fun to them.

"Thank you," I said to her, while reaching for the baby. "Did he eat?"

"Babe, of course he ate, several times, and I changed him, several times," she said half smiling.

"Thanks."

"Babe, what do you mean thanks? He's my son too."

Oh boy, why did she go there? I was trying to leave it alone but she had to go there. I'm gonna lose it.

"Your son? Where the fuck were you when they were cutting my ass open huh? Up under Suzanne's ass? You fucked up Zayle, big time this time!"

"I'm sorry Naia!"

"Sorry don't fucking cut it this time Zayle!"

Sivan starts to cry. I start to cry. She starts to cry. The only people that are getting any rest tonight in this house are the girls.

"Naia, please just get some rest and we will talk about this tomorrow, please."

"Tomorrow?"

"Yes, I took off the week to help out. I cancelled a few cases, I gave them to Malone at the firm."

As much as I wanted to stick to my pride and say hell no, I know that I need the help and I was exhausted. I told her thank you and turned around and headed to the kitchen. My breast were engorged so. I decide to make some bottles and go back to sleep.

I called Dahlia. "Hey girl."

"Hi Nai, I didn't want to call and take a chance and wake you, how are you?"

"I'm fine"

"How are the KIDS?" she said stressing kids.

I couldn't help but smile. "Their fine auntie Dee. Zayle is here."

"She is? I told you she would come around."

"Dee, coming around is not the problem...stability is, dependability is."

Her line beeped and she said that she would call me back. I welcomed the exit from this conversation. She was a fan of Zayle's and always wanted to use reason to validate everything.

This time I wanted to just go on emotions. I didn't bother waiting on her to click back over, I just decided to go and get some rest. I'm tired, I need some rest and right now I don't want to try and figure anything out. I made a choice to have my son and he is here, too late to turn back now.

I hung up the phone and walked back into the kitchen. Since she decided to stay over, I decided to make the best of it. I expressed my milk and sanitized the bottles and set them out for him. At three days old he was drinking milk every two hours and right on schedule. I needed to wash out a few things for him and the girls, but decided to wait until the weekend to do it. Let me get as much sleep as I possibly can right now.

I took a few bottles in the room so that Zayle would have them right beside her when he woke up, and the two of them were knocked out. She was sleeping so soundly that she didn't even hear that she had five missed calls. Right there on the screen readily for me to see was "Suzanne's" name.

I shook her and told her, "Hey, you better call Suzanne, she called you five times." She shrugged her shoulders and continued to sleep as if I didn't say anything at all. I personally was too tired to even care. I checked on the girls and went to sleep. Then it dawned on me. Everyone I love, is under one roof.

At least for now.

Chapter 26

I slept like a baby. By the time I woke up, Zayle had all ready gotten the girls off to school. The baby was already wiped up and smelling powdery fresh. I decided to go and tell her thank you but as I approached the door I could hear her whispering on her cell phone. I couldn't hear exactly what she was saying to the person but I decided to stand by the door and see if I could hear her.

Sivan started to cry so all I could hear her say was; "Babe, I told you that I was at my sister's house. Why would I lie to you?"

Is this bitch crazy? Oh lord I am gonna have to lose my mind and catch a fucking case! First of all not only is she denying our son but who is she is on the phone explaining herself to? The next I heard shut it all down. "Suzanne, I told you, I don't know who Anaya's baby is for or if she even had the kid, stop questioning me!"

With that I blasted into the room. I punched her straight in her face forgetting that the baby was in her arms. I don't know if I even cared. At this point I wanted blood. The nerve of this fucking girl, to even refer to our son as the "kid." Is she out of her fucking mind?

"NAI STOP!" "THE BABY IS IN MY HAND!"

"PUT HIM DOWN!" I yelled at her.

I started fighting her with everything that was inside of me. I pulled her hair and tried kicking her, completely forgetting that I had open stitches in my stomach.

She managed to get away from me and place Sivan in his bassinet. I kept coming at her and during it all I managed to pick her phone up off the side table and sailed it across the room not caring if it broke, that is exactly what I wanted. I wanted to smash it into pieces.

"Zayle who the fuck were you talking to?"

"Nai calm down! Be careful of your stitches ! That is not important who I was talking to."

"Oh really, that is what you think? I heard you Zayle. I heard what you said! Your sister's house?"

"Nai I didn't say that."

"Zayle are you trying to say that I am deaf, I heard you!" With all the commotion that was going on neither of us noticed that the door bell was ringing and that the person was also kicking the door.

"What the hell?"

"Naia, I'll get it."

"No the hell you won't! Who is it?"

No answer, just straight kicking at my door and my door bell ringing.

"WHO THE FUCK IS IT?"

I walk over and the fling the door open. All I remember was a fist coming at my face.

"YES BITCH! WHERE IS ZAYLE? I KNOW SHE IS HERE!"

It was Suzanne and I punched her dead in her face.

"FIRST THING FIRST, WHAT THE HELL ARE YOU DOING AT MY HOUSE SUZANNE?"
Zayle comes running into the room. "SUE!? WHAT THE HELL ARE YOU DOING HERE?"

"Zaye, don't ask that bitch no questions. I am about to rip her ass in two. How dare you come to my fucking house? Are you crazy?"

With that I rushed at her and kicked her straight in her chest, she flew backwards and then got up and charged at me. I grabbed her by her hair and proceeded to try and kick her in her head. I felt a sharp pain in my stomach, and doubled over in pain.

Zayle tried to grab me and pull me up and that is when Suzanne tried to grab me and get a hit off of me. Zayle came running over and grabbed her off of me.

"Zayle you're a fucking liar!" Suzanne is now screaming at Zayle and trying to grab after her.

"Listen, you and Zayle get the hell out of my house before you wake my son up!" Before I could say anything else, Zayle grabbed Suzanne and started pushing her out of the door. Oh my god what the fuck am I going to do? I can't believe this fucking girl is denying my son to this bitch that used all of her money, and doesn't even love her. Shit even worse she isn't supposed to love her so she says, so why is she denying my child.

"Zayle I told you from before I don't want any fucking drama in my life. Leave me and my son the hell alone! Go and be with Suzanne."

She starts trying to explain herself to me. Meanwhile Suzanne is steady kicking at my door and screaming as loud as she can calling me a whore.

"Zayle, I am going to call the cops on that bitch! I suggest you get your shit and take her home."

I can't believe this shit. This is worse than any heterosexual relationship I ever had. She walks over to me and tries to hug me? I pushed her straight off of me and into the table. Everything broke. Shit, I thought I killed her because blood was everywhere.

"Look what the fuck you made me do!" I ran and placed Sivan in the bassinet and ran over to her. She was just trying to get up and level out herself. I ran over to her. "Zayle I am sorry, I am so sorry, you know I am not a violent person."

I took her into the kitchen and examined her head to see if we would have to go to the hospital. Fortunately, it was a flesh wound. I asked her if she wanted to go to the hospital anyway to at least make sure that she didn't have a concussion, but she refused.

"Nai, I know you didn't mean to hurt me."

"No, I didn't, but you know how I feel about my children.

No one and I do mean NO ONE disrespects them Zayle! You know I will go to jail for my kids! You violated Sivan tonight, please leave."

I turned my back to walk away. The only thing that I was willing to do at this point was place a steri-strip on her wound and escort her out of my house.

"Zayle please leave, for the love of God before I lose it in here."

"Can I at least kiss my son, before I leave?"

"Yes, only because this will be the last time, you ever lay eyes on him", with that I walked over to the bassinet picked him up and handed him to her. I know that it was killing her. He looked exactly like her, and since she would never ever have her own biological child, and Ian already said that he would never inseminate anyone else this was it. Sivan...

See, Ian and her made a deal when she first came "out" to her family. He agreed that he loved her so much, that he would help her to have a child maybe two, if she was settled in a monogamous relationship. The limit was two, because he planned on having his own family, and the greatest thing of the arrangement was that they were fraternal twins. How perfect could that be for anyone? Even better, was the fact that I knew Ian myself and we were friends. When we approached him, he didn't even think twice.

She stood there holding him for a few minutes crying. Her tears wet his face, and woke him up. Him being the peaceful child that he is just looked up at her, and started to coo.

That must have broken her heart, because she started to cry even harder.

"Look at what your giving up Zayle, your five day old son."
I walk over and take him out of her hands.

She walked over to me bent over kissed us both and walked out. I was tempted to tell her to please not leave, except I couldn't. I wouldn't ask a man not to walk out on me, and I am damn sure, not going to ask a woman to not walk out on me.

I heard the door slam. I couldn't take it anymore. I put Sivan to lay on the bed and slumped to the floor and started to cry. What have I gotten myself into? Any normal girl, who fell in love with a girl, would not have gone to the extreme of having a child with them, what the fuck is wrong with me? Why do I have to go the extra mile? And to make it worse, she is just like any other man out there. You would think because she is a female she would at least think about things from a female point of view, at least sometimes. I mean God damn it I just had a child, is there any part of her that is feminine?

My head hurts, my body hurts and I can't stop crying. Sivan starts to cry and I can't even get up and tend to him. I want to die. I am so embarrassed and my heart is broken. How could I? How did I get played by a WOMAN? A fucking woman?

She is not supposed to outsmart me! I am supposed to know all the games that she could even think of playing; isn't it supposed to be easier, being in a relationship with a female? We think alike, don't we? Don't we want the same things? To be loved unconditionally? Didn't I show her unconditional love?

Sivan is now hollering his little lungs out. God I wish the girls were here so one of them could just hold him for me because I can't stop crying. I crawl into the bathroom. Look at me I am an emotional mess and a loser. My ex-man left me without warning for another woman.

He started a whole new life while still living with me. The woman, who I fell for and let down my guard with, has her own life and is denying me and a child that I had for her.

I look in the medicine cabinet and take out the bottle of Oxycodone that they gave me after the c-section. I reach into the medicine cabinet to get my anxiety pills. Maybe I should just end it all. End the hurt and the pain. It is bad enough that I am going to have to deal with my mother after I confess to her that yes, I really was with a woman all this time. Yes it was Zayle, and oh yeah by the way I had the baby with her.

The few friends that I had really didn't care one way or the other. They loved Zayle when I loved her and hated her when I hated her. They all tried to tell me that I would end up getting hurt but they supported my decision regardless.
 My house phone started to ring and I could hear the Caller ID announce Dahlia's cell phone number, I didn't answer and the answering machine picked up, "Hey sis, I am in the neighborhood. Are you up for company?"

I contemplated should I answer and take the pills while she is on her way? At least then Sivan won't have to suffer. He has already been crying for at least five minutes. I hear my son crying and can't even shake this feeling not to go and get him. Now I know I deserve to die. Over a woman? I am feeling this way over a fucking woman?

I crawl over to the bed and pick up my son. He didn't deserve this no matter what. He didn't deserve to be treated like this because he didn't ask to be here. I literally asked for him to be here and she asked for him to be here. God has the strangest way of letting you know that everything is going to be all right. As I was holding him, Sivan started to latch on to my breast to feed. He immediately settled down and stopped crying. He wrapped his tiny hands around my finger and moments later my girls called me to see how their baby brother was doing.

Hearing their voices brought me back to my senses. How could I? How could I have even entertained the thought of leaving my girls? Leaving my son? I am all that they have. So what their dad left me? It was his loss not ours. So what Zayle left me? Also her loss not mine. I made the choice to have my kids, now I have to show them how to be strong, to be humble, to prosper and go forward after any struggle.

I have to show them how to be....A PHOENIX.

Here's a sneak preview of

IN THE EYE OF THE STORM
By Brooklyn Phoenix
Book 2 of the Compilation

Want to find out what's next with Brooklyns Phoenix? Log onto:
www.brooklynsphoenix.com
Face Book   alteregopublishing yahoo.com
 www.myspace.com brooklynsphoenix
www.alteregopublishing.com

IN THE EYE OF THE STORM

It's been two weeks since I've moved into the new house. It feels a little different. I'm not use to so much space. It almost feels weird. Although this is what I've always wanted, I'm scared and lonely. My girls love their new house. They run up and down the stairs, even promising Sivan that when he gets older they will help him learn to slide down the banister.

It's just my children and I in this beautiful home. Work is good since I am now a full time partner at the pediatric office, and am even considering going solo into my own pediatric practice. I figure I will consider all of those options after I return to work from maternity leave.

Its 7:30 a.m. and the girls have to get on the school bus in ten minutes. I'm running around trying to get them ready to go out of the door and tend to my newborn baby. Nothing has changed with Darren since he still calls when he feels like calling and since I fought Suzanne, I haven't seen Zayle.

"Girls, let's go! The bus is outside!"

"Mommy, why can't you take us? Please?"

"Sweetie, I'll pick you guys up one day this week ok?"

I watch them go on the bus and run back inside. The baby is still sleeping thank God, so now I can at least try to finish unpacking. Sivan still hasn't gotten any form of a sleeping pattern, but hey he's entitled, he's only two weeks. He's so beautiful. Ian is coming by to visit and help me get some last minute painting done.

I asked him to please not give Zayle my new address. I decided it's best for me to take a nap until he wakes up, no point in driving my self into exhaustion.

A loud knock on my door awakened me out of my sleep. I thought I was dreaming until I heard my name.

" ANNAIYAH ! ANNAIYAH! I KNOW YOU'RE IN THERE!"

Who the fuck could that really be 9 in the morning calling my name out like a mad person? The neighborhood is so quite, it was almost echoing.

"ANAIYAH I KNOW YOUR FUCKING IN THERE!"

I slowly approach the door, and peek, only to see Darren.
I open the door, "What the hell is wrong with you? Why are you yelling my name out like that?"

"You fucking BITCH! I knew you were fucking that dyke bitch I always saw you with?"

"What? Darren what are you talking about?" See as far as I was concerned Darren didn't need to know my business. He cheated on me, had a child with another woman in Long Island and a home.

"Excuse me, what are you talking about?"

"Annaiyah, stop the fucking lying! Didn't you have her brother's baby? Didn't you go to Washington and catch her with her girlfriend!"

How the fuck does he know all of this?

"Didn't her girl just come to your apartment to fuck you up last week, what's her name Suzanne, and her name is Zayle, she is a lawyer in Brooklyn!"

How the fuck does he know all of this? Oh shit someone had to be telling him everything, but who?

"Yeah Naiyah , stand there like you don't know what the fuck I am talking about. You had this bitch around my girls, and your nastiness?"

"Darren get the fuck out my house, I don't owe you no explanation, go ask your bitch in your house about her life!"

With that he swung at me. "Are you out of your fucking mind Darren?! Get out before I call the cops and have you fucking arrested!"

"That's all right bitch, you can stay with your nasty bitch, but I'll make sure your mother and everyone at your job knows what kind of a nasty person you are. Tell your bitch, stay away from my kids, matter of fact I'll call her myself!"

"You do that Darren, since your God!"

"Oh don't worry I will! Her number is 347-555-6784!"
 What the fuck?

With that I rushed him out my door, and slammed my door shut behind him. I run to the phone and dial Dahlia. Dahlia was my Ace; I know she wouldn't betray me. Would she? Why would she? We've been friends since elementary school, why would she do that?

She knew I didn't want anyone to know. But then again she was the only one that had all the details that he was giving me. I didn't speak to anyone else the way I spoke to her. Did I?

I'm sitting on my couch trying to figure out, who could have possibly given him all this information about me and why? Everyone knew he cheated on me! They knew he had a whole separate life while he was living with me. So why would they betray me? I wasn't the bad guy.

My phone rings and it's my mother. I'm not going to answer I have to handle this situation first. The answering machine comes on and I can hear her loud and clear. "Annaiyah this is your mother, I need to speak with you. Is what I'm hearing

True? Were you really in a relationship with that girl? I'm so embarrassed call me back. Naiyah I'm letting you know right now if it is true, I am disowning you! Forget I'm your mother, and never call me again!"

Is this shit really happening?

I call Dahlia, no answer, "Dee, call me it's extremely important!"

The baby wakes up and I have to deal with him, at the same time I'm still trying to figure out who betrayed me? The phone rings and its Darren. Hell no I'm not answering! His voice comes over the machine, "That's why your dumb ass got raped, you stupid bitch!"

Oh my GOD! How the fuck does he know all of this?

Is Dahlia my Judus?   Even Judus kissed Jesus, before he handed him over.

Who's my Judus?

TM

Alter Ego Publishing
1800-403-8129

www.alteregopublishing.com

www.ingramcontent.com/pod-product-compliance
Lightning Source LLC
Chambersburg PA
CBHW020515120726
47904CB00003B/844